SPIRA MIRABILIS FANTASTIC TALES FROM THE MARVELOUS SPIRAL

RALPH SEVUSH

Spira Mirablis
Fantastic Tales from the Marvelous Spiral

By Ralph Sevush
Copyright © 2016 by Ralph Sevush.
All rights reserved.

Illustrations by Susan Kaufman
Copyright © 2015 by Susan Kaufman.
All rights reserved.

Published by taQ'Lut Press
First Printing: October, 2016

Layout, design and cover art: Joey Stocks
Proofreading: Tari Stratton

To

My parents, Norma & Dave,
Who started me on the journey,

My brothers, Herb and Steve,
For not smothering me in my crib,

My children, Jamie and Matthew,
For giving me a reason every day,

And to my beloved wife, Tobe,
Who has endured more than any wife should have to,

This book is lovingly dedicated.

Introduction

"Spira Mirabilis, Latin for "miraculous" or "marvelous" spiral—this name was given to the logarithmic curve by mathematician Jakob Bernoulli, because he was fascinated by one of its unique mathematical properties: the size of the spiral increases but its shape is unaltered with each successive curve. Possibly as a result of this unique property, the Spira Mirabilis has evolved in nature, appearing in certain forms such as conch shells, the pattern of approach taken by a hawk to its prey; and the arms of spiral galaxies and tropical cyclones, such as hurricanes." -- Wikipedia

Myths arise in different contexts throughout human history. They expand out and change, yet, like the Spira Mirabilis, they remain essentially the same. And this is likely so because WE remain essentially the same, give or take a millennium. Whether in an isolated aboriginal society or in a multicultural metropolis, we spin stories throughout time that are similar, despite their differences in local tailoring. Why? Perhaps we are hard-wired for it. After all, our self-awareness is one of our defining traits as a species. Perhaps we have evolved because of an innate need to bring order out of chaos, to find meaning in random occurrence, and to understand our place in the universe.

Stories are one of the ways we explain ourselves to ourselves. We thirst for them. So, to quench your thirst if only for a moment, I offer the eight tales in this compendium. Most of them are based on the recurring, varying yet constant motifs of the warrior hero, mixing ancient myths with genres of more recent origin, and pouring the concoction into new bottles. They're funny, violent and romantic in different proportions, like good stories of this type should be. But they are also about the act of telling the story, and the storyteller, too. For it is both in the giving and accepting of the tale that we discover who and what we are.

A final note about Jakob Bernoulli:

On his deathbed, Bernoulli requested that the figure of a logarithmic spiral, the Spira Mirabilis, be engraved on his tombstone, along with the Latin phrase: *"eadem mutata resurgo."* ("changed and yet the same, I rise again"). Inadvertently, the stonemasons carved a standard Archimedean spiral instead, and Bernoulli's stone remains that way to this very day. And in this cruel cosmic joke, we can see the damage that can be done by an indifferent storyteller who misses the truth of his tale even as he carves it in stone.

But, in my recounting of this incident, perhaps I am recasting Bernoulli's legacy the tiniest bit, reclaiming some fragment of him from the stonemason's lying chisel. Or, perhaps, I am merely engaging your attention for a brief moment, as you go from here to there, offering you a rip, a snort and a giggle along the way...but if you're lucky, and if I'm good, then maybe both.

Well, that's my story, at least, and I'm sticking to it.

Now, proceed.

Loewenstein awaits within...

"Things need not have happened to be true. Tales and dreams are the shadow-truths that will endure when mere facts are dust and ashes, and forgot."

— Neil Gaiman

TABLE OF CONTENTS

"I grab him by the throat and squeeze his words until he gags
on them. Then, I shove that fancy pig-sticker right into his
chest, quick as a schoolboy's squirt."

Emmett,
Joey, & the Beelz

EMMETT'S STORY

S o there I was, in yet another brawl
at Muldoon's Bar-n-Grill. And while
the joker swingin' the bike chain
was trying to indenture my skull, Joey
was still over by the bar, chattin' up some
pickled geezer, yammering on and on about
quantum mechanics.

"You can never know where sub-
atomic particles really are," is what Joey
was sayin', in his usual shpiel. "All you
can figure out are the odds that they're in
some given range of locations. And, since

people are made up of sub-atomic particles, then a person's reality is only probabilistic." Yada yada yada, blah blah blah.

Now I don't know much about quantum mechanics, but when the steel toe of that fat biker's jackboot kicked my jewels up into my throat, I felt like I was gonna puke out of my eye, and I knew Joey was wrong. There ain't nothin' probable about white-hot pain. It's simply a fact of life, and no poindexter's theory makes it hurt any less.

But I had it coming to me, anyways. I mean, you try and make time with a biker chick and you've gotta expect some pain in your life, one way or another. You generally don't expect to taste your nuts simply for complimenting a lady on her tattoo, but life is full of surprises. Besides, the fella apologized later. I think he realized he might've overreacted a little, and probably felt bad about it. He felt especially bad when I stuck the business end of my .38 deep into his nose and made him sing "Barnacle Bill the Sailor." Then, I joined in—me and Joey both—and we all had a grand time.

After that, the fella with the high-caliber nasal passages, well him and me got to chatting too, all friendly like. We talked baseball...well, we talked about the Mets which I guess is technically still baseball. And then we started comparing our tattoos; even Joey showed off that weird little thingy on his chest that he don't even remember getting. It looks like a pregnant snake giving a blowjob to a yak.

Joey likes to laugh at the one I got on my arm, up by my shoulder. It's my name, misspelled by some drunken *artiste*. I don't remember getting it either. But I kind of like that tat. It reminds me the stupid stuff I do when I get drunk. And I need reminding, from time to time.

Anyways, the next day, Joey found me while I was making my rounds. "Hey, Emmett," he says, "get your fat ass over here. I have news." Here he was, right on time, looking for his morning fix. But today he was all excited, just like he used to get in the old days, like he had a tip for me that would keep him in smack for weeks.

"Calm yourself, Joseph," says I, all businesslike. "What's got you hopping, hoppy?"

"I have news about Beelz," says he, real quiet.

When Joey said that, I just kept walking. I mean, here we were, standing on the corner of Avenue C and East Third, and this junkie says "Beelz" to me, just like that, just like nothing. What a bobo. Someday, I'm gonna scrape Joey off the bottom of my shoe and that'll be that. But for now, I think I'll just head back to Muldoon's. I need an eye-opener... bad.

THE JOURNAL OF JUDAH LOEWE

The great Rabbi Bezalel has finally completed my training. He has imparted to me his knowledge of the mystical arts and secret alchemies of Cabbala, deciphered from the sacred book...the *Book of Splendor*, the *Sefer Yetzirah*, the *Zohar*. "It is said by some that the Zohar was written by the hand of God, revealing Yahweh's secrets for the creation of life. Others say that Bezalel wrote the sacred book himself; that he is really a being as old as our faith, existing throughout time as an eternal aspect of the mind of God. But wiser men say nothing at all, as these things should not be spoken of.

– From the journal of Judah Loewe, Rabbi of Prague, 1582

JOEY'S STORY

The big, sweaty lummox that is Emmett Kowalchuk used to be of value to me when he wore a badge. He was powerful, amoral, and unrelenting. He was also an alcoholic of megalithic proportions...a propensity that made it necessary, in the end, that he be removed from his position as an agent of law enforcement.

I did have something to do with his downfall. But I really don't want to talk about that. Actually, I can't because I've scorched the details from my mind, but let's just say we all do things of which we are later ashamed. Like becoming associated with that dark creature Emmett calls "da Beelz." And no, I will not discuss that now either, thank you very much.

Once upon a time, I taught mathematics to the snotty scions of New England. I lived a quiet and solitary existence on an island of old money from whence I had already started to drift. Then I left the old world behind and sailed off on the deep dark waters of the urban sea. When the tide withdrew, I had washed up in Hell and had no way home. So I swam back out into the strong current, hoping to be pulled under...and I was. I float now, from shadow dream to fevered nightmare and back again.

I still read quite a bit, though. Not my special book, of course. I have that one hidden away for a rainy day. No, now it's mostly pornographic comic books featuring young Asian girls being raped by robots. My attention span doesn't permit me much more. I recently tried re-reading Camus' *L'Étranger*, but I discovered that I could no longer read French. The words were just squiggly lines on the page, twisting and cavorting for no apparent reason and I couldn't seem to make them stop.

So, Camus, and Pollack, and Stravinsky, and Heisenberg—and anyone I ever loved or whoever loved me—have all been replaced by a syringe. And by Emmett...that lumbering fool Emmett, who seems like he's always been right there next to me in the shadows. And now he keeps me fixed, as the need arises. God knows why. Guilt, maybe. Or maybe he thinks we're friends. Maybe he thinks he's doing me a favor. Or maybe he's just trying to kill me.

EMMETT'S STORY, CONTINUED

Muldoon's is owned by this fellow heeb I know, old Saul Muldoon, and he has this slightly retarded fella, Jesus, who cleans up and sleeps in the bar to look after things. Jesus pours me a shot of JD with a raw egg every morning and gives me a place to be for a while. In return, I provide some services for the old man...debt retrieval services.

Joey won't let up this morning, what with this Beelz crap, so I get him loaded and off to La-La Land he goes, stretched out on Jesus' cot. As for me, I stare down at the egg in my Jack and it's staring back at me like the yellow eye I popped out of somebody's head once, down on Canal. What was that guy's name? Eddie. Eddie Phlegner. Always had that runny, rheumy, yellow eye...'til I popped it out. That was back in my bad days, back when I first met the Beelz. I was out of control, easy to piss off, and hard to buy back then. Lots of bourbon under the bridge and over the dam since, and a lot has changed. Ya see, I'm pretty easy to buy now.

The Beelz bought me once, I sorta remember. The price wasn't that high and he paid it easy, and then he owned me. Still does, I guess. I'm not sure anymore about the details. And if he's back looking for me, my life has just gotten nastier.

Hell, I been shot, stabbed, worked over with a tire iron, and run over by a Cadillac doing eighty through my living room, and I ain't dead yet. But Beelz...keee-riest.

Okay, stop your bellyaching, Emmett. Mama Kowalchuk didn't raise no whiner. And at least shit-storms are exciting.

Emmett & Joey: A Conversation

"Up, Joseph. Up!" I haul Joey up from Jesus' cot and lean him against the end of the bar. His body sags and his head flops over, like a puppet with its strings cut.

"Emmett, Emmett, go away, come again some other day," he singsongs.

"'Beelz', Joey. You said 'Beelz' to me. Right out there on the street. So now you have to pull yourself together and start talking, lest you want me to hafta beat it out of you, like the old days. Cuz if you're getting nostalgic on me, hoppy, I'll be happy to oblige."

Joey blinks, like he's trying to focus. "Beelz...yes...but now I'm having such a lovely hallucination, so could you just—"

"Sorry, Joe. You been there and I done that. Now I need to start making plans. For plans, I need the 411. You seem to know something, so now I need to know it too." I grab his collar and pull his face up to mine, close enough he could floss with my nose hairs. "Otherwise, I'll just put you down like the sick dog you are and high tail it to the hinterlands. Staten Island, maybe."

I guess I hit a nerve because Joey perks right up. "Yes, right, Mr. Kowalchuk. Beelz would never find you in that landfill masquerading as a borough. In fact, with your stench you'll fit right into that compost heap of a—uhhh!"

"That, Joseph, as you may remember, was my short left jab. If you want the hard right cross, just keep stalling."

"Emmett, may I have a napkin please?" A trail of blood and snot runs down Joey's face.

I swipe a pile of cocktail napkins from up on the bar and throw them at him.

"Here."

"Thank you," he mumbles as he wipes his nose.

"Don't mention it."

"Where were we?"

"Beelz," I say, with the *z* rattling through my gritted teeth.

Joey takes a long breath. "Some of my, um, compatriots have seen a long black stretch limo creeping around the neighborhood. They saw it slow down one time, to ask one of the boys a question. A door opened, the guy was pulled in, and the car sped off. At least that's what I heard."

"A junkie disappeared into the back of a black stretch limo?"

"Yes."

"And that's IT?"

"No. The license plate. It was BZL–777, from out of state."

"And you think that was da Beelz?"

"Well, who else? Don't you see? He's finally tracking us down! He wants his payment, or whatever."

I let go of Joey's collar. "Bullshit, Joe," I say, not sure at all that it's bullshit.

"Fine. I just thought you should know. So now you do. It's nothing to me if you're not going to do anything about—"

"More bullshit. You just want me to cover your ass. Just like always."

"And so? After all I've done for you?" Joey looks away and wipes his nose again.

"All you done for...." I can taste bile, so I stop talking. "You know, sometimes I just wanna put a pillow over your face, pull out my piece, and put a nice, quiet hole right in the middle of that skeevy mug of yours."

Joey goes limp. "Well, sometimes...sometimes I want that, too."

"Yeah. Well. Anyway, I'll check into the limo thing. It's probably just some junkie behind in his payments, so some Columbians took him for a joyride. But I'll check it out, just to put your mind at ease. Okay?

"If it is Beelz, we're going to have to move quickly and quietly. Otherwise he's going to come and send us straight to Hell."

I stand up. "I'm a Jew. We don't believe in Hell. It would be, whaddyacall, redundant."

Joey looks up, with his puppy dog eyes. "You know exactly what—"

"Just stay outta sight for a while. Don't go to your usual alleys. Stay away from your flop and mine. We'll both stay away from Muldoon's, too."

"You sound like you're starting to take this seriously."

"Well, better play it safe til we know."

Joey starts to shake a little. "If you go to Staten Island without me, I...I don't know what I'll—"

"Easy there, little man. I ain't been run outta town yet. I'm too old, fat, and slow to run that far anyway."

"Please, just...just don't leave me here...alone."

"Find a new hole." I help Joey to his feet. "When the coast is clear, I'll come get you."

Joey holds onto the edge of the bar. "Give me your word."

"Yeah, okay. For whatever that's worth."

"Thank you, Emmett."

"Don't sweat it, Joseph."

EMMETT, ALICE & DONALD R. BELZAHN, ESQ.: TWO CONVERSATIONS

(*Ring...ring...ring.*)

"Mr. Kowalchuk's office."

"Mr. Kowalchuk, please."

"Whom shall I say is calling?"

"Donald R. Belzahn, attorney at law, calling on behalf of my client, Dr. Abrahim Bezalel."

"I'm sorry but Mr. Kowalchuk is not currently available. Would you like to leave a message?"

"Thank you, miss. Please let him know that my client has asked me to negotiate with Mr. Kowalchuk regarding the final terms of their arrangement."

"Would you like to leave a number where you can be reached, Mr. Belzahn?"

"No. I'll get a hold of Mr. Kowalchuk at some other time. Thank you. Have a nice day."

(*Click.*)

"Thanks Alice. That was perfect." I stretch out under the covers.

"No sweat, Emmie." Alice is chewing her gum like she means it. "So you're forwarding all your calls here now?"

"Just for a little while, 'til this blows over. And change the message on your answering machine, okay?"

"Sure. Okay. For ten bucks."

"Ten?"

"A day."

"A DAY?" I sit up so quick I hit my head on the shelf above the bed. "You mean, on top of—"

"Yeah." She pops her gum in my face. "On top."

"Okay."

"One week in advance, payable now." She holds out her hand.

"Yeah, yeah, okay." I already knew Alice could screw a guy six ways from Sunday, but this was the seventh. I pull my pants off the floor and check through my pockets. I find a handful of sawbucks and toss them at her. "Here."

She snatches the bills out of the air, counts up the money, and right away turns cheerful. "Thanks, Em. Gee, I'm sure sorry to hear you've got a lawyer after you. That sucks. Those guys are pit-bulls, you know."

"Alice, you have no idea. I'm stuck between the Devil and the Deep Blue Sea. Now come back to bed, sweet-cheeks. I've still got three minutes left on the meter."

"Ooooh, you sweet-talker (*giggle*)."

EMMETT'S STORY, CONTINUED

Well, I just got saved a lot of wear and tear on my old gumshoes. It seems Joey was right. The Beelz was back, and he was looking for us. With Belzahn, yet. Crap. But I guess I shoulda seen that coming because the Beelz always said that, when the end came, he'd be there...with Belzahn.

I was probably being watched right this second. Here, and at Muldoon's, and at Joey's hole.. everywhere. Everywhere I usually go I couldn't go no more. Phones are probably tapped, too. And Alice—my sweet whore, Alice— she's probably maybe the one that tipped Beelz, and then she took my seventy bucks just as an extra kick in the head. Maybe I should snap her neck like a dry twig, but aw, why bother? She's a good kid and, either way, I'm gonna have to haul ass.

And Joey. I should find Joey. Or maybe not. Maybe there's no time to worry about that ferret anymore. Every man for hisself, maybe. Damn, this old tattoo is starting to itch like crazy.

JOEY'S STORY, CONTINUED

"Hi, this is Alice Niedermeyer. You've reached the offices of Kowalchuk Investigations. Please leave a message at the tone...(*giggle*). Have a nice day!" (*Beep.*)

"Hello, Emmett? I know you're there. Pickup. Pickup. PICKUP PICKUP PICKUP! This is no time to have a whore screening your calls, you fat, stupid, kike bastard! Ok, ok. Emmett, please. Please pick up the phone. I'm sorry. I won't call you fat anymore, I promise. Only please pick up the phone." (*Beeeeep.*) (*Click.*)

He's gone. I bet he just took off, without a word or a how-do-you-do. I knew he would, promise or no promise. In the end I always knew I'd be alone, utterly and completely alone, waiting for Beelz to collect me. And now it's time and here I am, with only a rash on my damn tattoo for company.

I saw the black limo again. It may have seen me, too. I'm not sure. But I saw it. It's real. Not some opiated fever dream, but really real.

You know something? Wisconsin is nice this time of year. Almost as nice as New Hampshire, in fact. In Wisconsin, they've got cheese and other dairy products, and cows that give milk as sweet as the girls milking them—big, healthy, blonde, corn-fed, Aryan girls—and lakes, deep and clear, surrounded by green fields. Madison. Madison, Wisconsin is a nice college town. Maybe I can get a job there again. But I can't walk to Wisconsin. The ulcers on my feet wouldn't get me past Hoboken. And that damn book is too damn heavy to carry that far.

Maybe I could make it back to New Hampshire. I bet I still have relatives there, somewhere. But I'd never get past their security gates.

In point of fact, it would seem my options are fairly limited. It's either kill myself or...wait a second. Wait, wait, wait; it's really Emmett that Beelz wants, isn't it? I mean, technically, I was part of the deal, too, I think—I'm still kind of hazy on the details—but if I can set up Kowalchuk for him, maybe I can get out of this. After all, it's every man for himself and, as Fassbinder noted, God against all.

Joey & Belzahn: A Conversation

"Mr. Belzahn?" I query, tremulously, into the phone.

A smooth voice replies, drowning the static. "Yes?"

"This is Joey... um, Joe. Joseph. Mr. Joseph Low." I swallow and lean my head against the grimy phone booth. "I hear you've been looking for me. I mean, that is, Mr. Beelz has."

"Doctor Bezalel has given me instructions to close the deal, Mr. Loewe. So, why don't you make it easier for everybody and come down to my office and we'll—"

"I've got a new deal to make, Mr. Belzahn."

"Really? Well, I don't think Dr. Bezalel would be at all—"

"I'll give you Emmett Kowalchuk on a silver platter, without a fuss."

"Yes, well, that's nice, but I think we can handle—"

"And...and the book. I can get you the book."

"The book? Really?"

"In exchange for a free pass."

There is a pause on the other end of the line. "I see."

I clear my throat. "And carfare to Wisconsin."

"Wisconsin?"

"Madison, Wisconsin. Yes."

Static crackles during another pause. "Yes. I see."

"Well?"

"Well, I'll take your offer to my client. He might be interested. We'll see, Mr. Loewe. I can't make you any promises, you understand."

"I understand, Mr. Belzahn," I reply with feigned dignity.

"Give me your number and I'll call you back tomorrow morning," he says.

I stare at the receiver, lying there, cold in my sweaty hand. "Well, I'm between phones right now. I'll call YOU tomorrow. Around 9 a.m.?"

"That'll be fine, Judah. You have my number, apparently."

"Yes, I do. And my name isn't Judah. It's... (*Click. Bzzzzz.*) ...Joe."

Rabbi Loewe & the Golem of Prague

The following is excerpted from *Golem Stories* by Professor Josiah Loewenstein (Wisconsin University Press):

...but wiser men say nothing at all, as these things should not be spoken of.

– From the journal of Judah Loewe, Rabbi of Prague, 1582

And it came to pass that Loewe, who was a good and decent man, heard the cries of his people, the Jews of Prague, who were decimated by hate, by deprivation, by pogrom. He studied the sacred *Zohar* to find their salvation and, after many days and nights, he attempted the creation of a golem...a soulless creature in the figure of a man, shaped from simple clay. It would offer his people their only hope of survival.

Joey's Story, continued

I shouldn't have done it. Every inch of my mottled flesh screamed a warning to me, to avoid this obvious setup. But what choice did I have, really? Beelz would find me eventually and I would then be at the old man's mercy. This way, I meet with him on my terms, and if I live long enough to make a deal, I might live long enough to regret it thereafter. To live with regret, after all, is still to live. Even in Wisconsin.

The next morning, I, um, ran some errands. Then I met the limo at the corner of Avenue C and East Sixth Street, around 3 p.m. When I got in, the tinted glass left me in semi-darkness and blind as to who was driving. For all I knew, there was no driver.

The car finally stops in front of the synagogue up on Fifth Avenue... an elegant establishment where the regulars pay extra to sit closer to God on the High Holy Days. I stumble out of the dark car, into the bright light of the late afternoon. Despite the heat of the sun, an intense chill runs through my body.

I can see Belzahn waiting for me on the marble stairs that lead up to the temple's massive doors. He leads me inside, where I'm suddenly frozen by the light streaming through the Chagall windows from above; the deep reds of the stained glass put me in mind of the blood of the innocents, spilled over and over throughout time, and the light blues recall the sky as seen by a sea of dead and empty eyes, staring lifelessly up from their mass graves.

We enter a private room off the vestibule just inside the doors. There sits Bezalel, unchanged since I last saw him...when, seven years ago? His long beard partly obscures his white, dapper seersucker suit, off the rack from another time and place. He wears the same black derby and smokes a cigar. His blue, blue eyes match the stained glass windows, and they gleam with some inner fire.

Bezalel begins.

"Hello, Judah. Good to see you."

"Hello, Doctor. Um, it's Joseph, not Judah. Surely you must remember."

"Indeed I do." He smiles, baring sharp white teeth.

"Um. Yes. Well, you look the same."

"Yes. But you look different, Judah. Older. And something else besides."

"Scared," I offer, with utmost sincerity.

"No, you were always scared, Judah. Worn away, perhaps."

"Yes, perhaps." Why doesn't he just get on with it?

Belzahn interjects. "The book, Mr. Loewe? You said you could deliver the book."

The good doctor laughs. "Please, Belzahn. Mr. Loewe is just settling in. You see, Judah? Lawyers. Feh!"

"No, I understand, Doctor. He just wants to get down to business. I can respect that. It's just that I need certain assurances."

Bezalel smiles, almost kindly. "Of course, of course... but first, a gesture of good faith, yes? You must assist us in neutralizing *Emet*. Then the location of the book and the logistics of your freedom can be discussed in detail."

I am puzzled. "*Eh-MET*? Oh, you mean Emmett. Well, he'll not be easy to neutralize. He's a big, mean, drunken, heavily armed, soulless killing machine. And I have no idea where he is. Maybe Staten Island, but—"

"Emet remains soulless, still? That's so sad, Judah. Not wholly unexpected, but sad nonetheless. Your sacrifice was for naught, it seems."

"Sacrifice? What sacrifice? What was for naught?"

"Your deal with me."

"Well, I don't really remember the, um, exact terms of the deal, so—"

"Of course not. Neither does Emet. That was part of the deal, too."

"I'm not feeling well, Bezalel. Stop talking in circles."

Belzahn hands me a drink to steady me. I knock it back without thinking. It smells of flowers—I'm remembering lilacs, in a garden—and suddenly I'm spinning into a funnel, spiraling down. I wake up on the floor, with Belzahn sitting on top of me. He has a bejeweled dagger in his hand and I can't move. The drink has left me paralyzed.

Belzahn rips open my shirt. Without a moment of hesitation, he cuts the tattoo from my chest with a single parabolic swipe of his blade. I would scream if my throat could form words. Suddenly, a torrent of images floods my mind, as the world falls away and I circle back into memory.

RABBI LOEWE & THE GOLEM, CONTINUED

Loewe drew his charts, calculated his numbers, spoke his incantations, made his prayers and, with the elements of fire, water, wind and earth, fashioned a man out of the mud of the riverbank. No, not a man...a golem.

Onto its arm he carved the word *Emet*—"truth", in the ancient tongue. This would bind the creature to Loewe, giving him dominion over it. Seven times, the rabbi circled the golem...*Shanti, shanti, dahat, dahat,*" he said. Then, into its ear, Loewe whispered Yahweh's unspoken name.

And the golem opened its eyes.

Silent and mighty, the golem defended the Jews of Prague. But lacking a soul, the golem had no mercy, no compassion, no humanity. And in exercising a fierce vengeance, it became a monstrous, unstoppable killer.

EMMETT'S STORY, CONTINUED

I knew Joey would try something, so I let him try. I lifted Belzahn's phone number off Alice's Caller I.D., and then I made sure to joke about it with Joey. 555-0777? Hardee har har.

The next morning, I staked out Muldoon's and Joey showed up around ten, carrying that big book of his. I listened at the door as he talked at Jesus.

"Stay by the phone, Jesus. You might hear from me around three, four this afternoon. I might need you to bring this book to me. You understand?"

"Sure, Joey, I unnerstan."

"But, if you don't hear from me by, say, six, well, then burn the damn thing. Okay?"

"Sure, Joey, I burn."

"Good man. There will be a serious payday in this for you. Thanks."

"But what I tell Emmett?"

"Nothing. You tell him nothing."

"But Emmett is—"

"Nothing. You understand, Jesus?"

"Sure, Joey. I unnerstan."

After Joey left, I had a friendly little chat with Jesus. He was happy to turn the book over to me because, you see, I have a way with people. Then I picked up Joey's trail. He got loaded and nodded off for a while behind Hung Lo's Noodle Emporium, but around three that afternoon he hopped into a black limo at C and East Sixth and took off. Damn. Waddya know? There IS a black limo. I tossed the book into the backseat of my broken-down ragtop Eldorado and followed at a distance.

So now I'm double-parked up on ritzy Fifth Avenue, and I watch in the rearview as Joey and Belzahn go inside a big *shul* across the street. I sit and wait a while, thumbing through Joey's book. Fancy thingamajig, but it's all Babylonian to me. Meantime, I'm giving Joey a few more minutes to smoke out the Beelz, to get in good and deep, and then I guess I'll go save his ungrateful ass.

What I should be doing is high-tailing it over the Verrazano Bridge, pushing this old Eldorado as hard as she'll go. Past Staten Island, even. To Jersey, maybe...maybe even further than that. Just leave, without Joe, without the stink of this life covering me like a skunk coat. Just leave and don't look back. Not ever.

But no. Instead, I'm gonna go pull Joey's chestnuts out of an open fire. He wouldn't do it for me, probably. So, why? Well, maybe it's just because I promised him I would. For whatever that's worth. Because if your word don't mean anything, well then, hell, what kind of man are you?

RABBI LOEWE & THE GOLEM, CONTINUED

...but lacking a soul, the golem had no mercy, no compassion, no humanity. And in exercising a fierce vengeance, it became a monstrous, unstoppable killer.

So, Bezalel returned to Prague.

"Loewe, the golem must be stopped."

"Yes, master, I have lost control of it."

"Your control was an illusion from the outset."

"I see that now," admitted the young rabbi.

"Remove the sacred word from its arm with this dagger, and the creature shall return to dust," Bezalel advised, offering a knife the likes of which Loewe had never seen.

Loewe turned away. "But who will protect us then?"

"We are in God's hands, my son. As we have ever been."

"But Bezalel, I...I've lost my faith in God's protection. Don't you see? We must take steps to protect ourselves."

"Judah, a soulless creature is beyond any man's control."

"But... but what if... what if it had a soul? Surely then it could be our—"

"Our what? Our savior? The *Meshiach*?"

"Yes!"

"Blasphemy, Judah!"

"Perhaps so," whispered Loewe.

Bezalel pondered. "And how do you propose it gain this soul?"

"Master, you wrote the book. Surely, you could—"

"I wrote nothing, Loewe. I am merely a disciple, like yourself."

"Yes, Master. But isn't there anything in the sacred texts that could help us?"

"Within its pages can be found the answer to every question!"

Evincing a great and damning hubris, Bezalel opened the *Zohar* and poured over it throughout the night. Outside, the bodies of the righteous and un-righteous alike started stacking up like cords of wood, and the city of Prague became like a funeral pyre, its teeming stench reaching up to the heavens.

Finally, Bezalel emerged and spoke.

"Judah, the golem is connected to you. If I wipe clean your memory, its mind, too, will become a blank slate. And onto that slate, life may yet write a story that leads the golem to a soul. So, what say you?"

"But, master, what of my life? What of my people? And without my memories, how shall I guide the golem, how shall I advise it?"

"This is your decision, your sacrifice to make. I will tend to your congregation, but you must take your golem and go out into the world. You will teach it to speak, to live like a man. The spell I cast will grant you false memories, ever changing, so you might both survive the ages with your purpose intact. You will remember nothing but your debt to me, which will always seem but seven years past, as seven is the sacred number and the center of all things."

"But for how long, master?"

"A day will come, a day 420 years hence—measuring seven times a lifespan of three score years—when I shall return and seek you out. If by that time the golem has gained a soul, you shall be restored and live out your days in God's grace, and the golem will become the champion of our people. But if it remains what it is—a soulless creature, uncontrollable and unredeemed—then it shall be returned to the dust, and you shall join it."

Loewe sighed. "420 years... by that time, our people will be nothing but a memory."

"We will persevere, Loewe. We have always persevered."

Loewe walked to the window and stared out at the nightmarish spectacle of a violent world descending into chaos. His own silence deafened him.

Bezalel spoke once more. "So now, what say you, Rabbi Loewe of Prague?"

And Loewe whispered, "I will do what I can. What I must."

Bezalel then etched upon Loewe's chest a sacred glyph, a symbol that would cast the spell and hide the truth from Loewe through the ages to come, until the day it was removed. Loewe next found himself standing in a Czechoslovakian wheat field, beside his mute creation. They were heading down a road, unsure where they were going.

After a time, Emet turned to Loewe and said...

Emmett's Story, continued

"...hey, Joey, wake the fuck up!"

"Emet, what are you—where are—what is—?"

"You're laying here in a pool of blood and you're asking me questions? Where's that prick, Belzahn?" I ask, when, right at that moment, I hear the snake slither up behind me.

"Golem! Release your maker. Rise and face me," Belzahn hisses.

I sneak Joey the book and tell him to hide it. He tries to tuck it under his coat but it's too big, and I see the blood on Joey's chest, like he's been worked over with a straight edge. Slowly, I turn.

"Belzahn," I whisper, "you do this?"

Belzahn points a pretty impressive knife at me, smiles and says, "Yes, golem. And I'm not done yet."

I see something moving in the shadows, out of the corner of my eye. Ahhh, the Beelz finally shows his ugly mug. "Wait a moment, Belzahn," he says, "Lower the dagger. Let us welcome Emet home."

"First, Beelzie, I think you're gonna need to get yourself a new shyster," I say, as I pull my .38, wheel on Belzahn and fire three times point blank into his chest before anyone can even blink. Then the Beelz starts chanting, "shanti, shanti, dahat, dahat," and I—

JOEY'S STORY, CONTINUED

The golem suddenly freezes, its arm extended, its gun pointing in the air in an empty gesture of accusation. Belzahn just smiles his deathless grin as the bloodless holes across his torso instantly close. Bezalel then turns to face me as I stare up, helpless, from my prone position on the floor.

"Now, Judah. Come. Return the book that you have stolen. It is time to finish this."

RABBI LOEWE & THE GOLEM, CONCLUDED

For 420 years, Judah—now called Joseph—roamed the land with his hulking servant, now called Emmett. They farmed, they soldiered, they sold, traded, bartered, and built...they loved and they hated...they broke, they destroyed, they lied, stole, maimed and killed.

And every seven years they would begin again, without aging and without memory of the last turn of the wheel, but somehow changed with each incarnation. They walked through time, this man and his creature...like flying Dutchmen doomed to sail in search of something they knew not what.

One day, the road led them back to Bezalel, whom they now called "Beelz." They knew him. Hadn't they made some sort of deal with him only seven years ago? Before he could harm them, Joseph and Emmett succeeded in stealing from Beelz his prized possession: a book, overlarge, leather-bound and jewel-encrusted, with letters made from gold leaf, in ancient words that were undecipherable. They would hold it as leverage against Beelz, should their paths ever cross again.

But, as the years and centuries passed, the book's import slipped from their minds, as their minds slipped into madness and out again, one lifetime after another. They anesthetized themselves against their plight, and their degradation continued. And then, seven years after the sixtieth turn of the wheel, the final days came.

Joey's Story, contnued

I rise and hand the sacred *Zohar* to Bezalel. "I remember it all now, Master. So many years lost. Centuries burned away. My hopes, my prayers, my dreams...all unanswered. And for what? I've made nothing more of the golem than I first did all those years ago in Prague. And I've made so much less of myself."

Bezalel opens the book. "No recriminations now, my dear Judah. It is time to make an end. We must remove the *Emet* from the golem's arm, so that it may crumble back into the dust. But first the blade must be purified by fire, wind and water, so when it joins with the earthen clay of the golem's flesh, it is able to complete its task."

Bezalel takes the knife from Belzahn. Then, as Bezalel recites an incantation from the *Zohar*, blue flames burst forth from his blue, blue eyes and engulf the dagger in a fire that does not burn. When he reads a second passage, attorney Belzahn opens his mouth and releases a mysterious gust of hot air that blows through the chamber. Bezalel holds the knife aloft and its blade starts to gleam.

"First fire, then wind. Now water," the doctor says, putting his hand on my shoulder. When he reads a third passage from the Book of Wonder, I start to feel woozy and drop to my knees. Suddenly, all the bile and sickness I've absorbed through 420 years of misspent life come flowing up out of me in a torrent of fetid liquid, shooting out like a black fountain, retching out of me and onto the blade. I am cleansed, and the blade now glows with a bright white intensity. All is ready.

"Take the blade, Judah. Cut the word from the earthen flesh of the golem."

"I?"

"It was yours in the making. It must be yours in the unmaking. Go. Make an end."

He hands me the knife. I turn to face the golem. It is a creature I've known, through various incarnations, for a very long time. I made it with my own hands and with the best of intentions. In the end, it had even returned to save me, against all expectations. And now I'm going to destroy it. No, not *it...him*. I'm going to destroy HIM. *What kind of soul must I have to do such a thing*, I wonder.

"I'm so sorry, Emet...*Emmett* I mean. I'm sorry for everything," I whisper, raising the blade. His eyes stare into me with something approaching, what? Forgiveness?

I cut through Emmett's coat, ripping open the sleeve and the shirtsleeve beneath, exposing his tattooed flesh. I hesitate for only a moment, and then quickly slice the *Emet* from his arm. Blood pours forth. Blood? But how can a golem bleed?

EMMETT, JOEY & THE BEELZ

When I finally snap out of it, Joey is slicing off a chunk of my freakin' arm. So I snatch the knife away and toss him aside like a rag doll. Then, quick as a toe dancer on Crank, I spin and throw and bury the blade up to its hilt in Belzahn's forehead. He slumps to his knees with a surprised look on his face and he folds like a kangaroo straight in a game of Stud. He stares up at me from the cold stone floor, and that look on his face? Well, the memory of it is gonna give me the giggles for years, if I live for years.

Then I turn to the Beelz, who looks like he just shit hisself. You know, I don't remember ever seeing that wrinkled old bastard look scared before.

I raise my .38, throw the old fella a cute wink, and let loose with the lead. But for the second time today... nothing. The Beelz doesn't show a scratch on him. I stare down at my gun. "I gotta have this thing checked. It used to be pretty good at blowing the heads offa cock-suckers."

Beelz starts his chanting again—"shanti, shanti, dahat, dahat"—but this time it don't do squat to me. So I look over at Joe, who's still kinda freaked. "What now, hoppy?" I says.

Joey yelps, "The knife, Emmett! Get the knife!"

But as soon as I yank the knife out of Belzahn's skull, he pops back up like a Weeble and starts clutching at me, trying to pull the knife away. So I hack off his arm, slicing clean through at the shoulder. And as I'm standing there, holding his disconnectified wing, the rest of Donald R. Belzahn, Esquire, disintegrates into a pile of dust. Poof, just like that.

"Shanti, shanti," goes the Beelz. I use what's left of Belzahn's tattooed, still-solid arm to knock the Beelz upside his head, and I grab him by the throat and squeeze his words until he gags on them. Then, I shove that fancy pig-sticker right into his chest, quick as a schoolboy's squirt. But again, nothing. Shit! What do I gotta do to kill this old man?

"The book, Emmett! Destroy the book!" screams Joey. So I stick the shiv right into the middle of the book, and then—

JOEY'S STORY, CONCLUDED

A column of flame erupts from the wound in the sacred tome, knocking Emmett to the ground next to me, where I sat frozen. Bezalel, his eyes wide in disbelief, bursts into flame too, and his blue, blue fire intertwines with the red, red flames of the *Zohar* as the burning, smoking column shoots up through a sudden hole in the roof of the temple; up, up into the late afternoon sky.

And then, just as suddenly as the inferno roared to life, the flames are gone. The book drops to the floor, spent. Bezalel is no more. All that remains in the dimly lit chamber is blue and red light streaming through stained glass windows, filtered through the smoke hanging in the deathly still air.

Emmett turns to me and says, "Where'd he go, Joe?"

"He has returned to the mind of God, my friend," I reply.

We sit and stare into the smoke for a very long time.

EMMETT'S STORY, CONCLUDED

So there I was at Muldoon's, drinking a lukewarm Bud, eating some pickled eggs, and watching the Mets lose another one from my usual table, when Alice brought me over a package we just got in at the office. Yeah, I was still using her place as my office, and she was still screening my calls. She's a sweet kid, really, and she gives me a discount now, so what the hell.

Anyways, inside the package was a book with another postcard from Joey; this one had a picture of two smiling blondes, with their melons spilling out of their overalls, way too happy about milking a cow. Gee, now that Joey remembers that he's a Jew, I hope he remembers to keep his meat away from the dairy queens out there in Wisconsin.

So the postcard says:

Dear Emmett,

Just letting you know my book is finally getting published. I've dedicated it to you, by the way. I know you won't read it, but I'm sending it to you anyway.

With love,
Joe

A free copy, huh? Okay, Joseph. Free is good. Besides, it'll be nice to have a book around the office. It'll impress the clientele, for whatever that's worth. And I can always use it to kill those huge freakin' roaches living in Alice's stove.

So, I flip open the book. It's called *Golem Stories* by Josiah Loewenstein, and the dedication says:

"For Emmett–
With whom I walked a Mobius strip in time,
And from whom I learned that
Even the most improbable life

Can define itself through its deeds.
So have a good life, my friend, or a bad one...
Your choice.
Like they say in New Hampshire,
'Live free or die; death is not the worst of evils.'"

It's nice to hear from Joey every once in a while. Before he took off, he told me that, when I kept my word by coming to save him even after he tried to sell me out, I proved that I DID have a soul. Not too much sense of course, but a soul. So when he cut my tattoo off, I was freed, not fucked.

Well, I don't know about all that. But, I guess if I was still some golemmy-type thingamajig, I wouldn't be sitting here at my regular joint, with my very own girl, reading a postcard from my very own pal, and watching my very own Mets lose another one.

Ya see, if I was really some kind of soulless monster, well, hell...

...then I'd be a Yankee fan.

Emmett, Joey & the Beelz

The medication had just started to kick in, so I was no longer a palpable threat to my family. Still, I needed a creative release, so I returned to a literary form I had abandoned long ago—the short story.

I was reading a lot of Neil Gaiman's work at the time, and I had read Michael Chabon's *Amazing Adventures of Kavalier & Clay* some time earlier. I was also in the midst of a Jim Thompson pulp noir overload. With all that stuff still swimming in my head, I saw Michael Frayn's play *Copenhagen* and, when I came home that night, I wrote a paragraph about a tough guy in a bar fight who was thinking about the Heisenberg Uncertainty Principle.

When I had originally written that paragraph, the tough guy seemed a combination of Ralph Meeker in *Kiss Me Deadly* and Benjamin Grimm, the ever-lovin' blue-eyed Thing, but I had no idea who he was or who he was talking to, or why. But when I returned to that paragraph some years later, I finally understood that he was a golem (Thank you, Mr. Chabon). Once I had the golem, I had a mythology to research, which gave me a lot of stuff to read and think about, and a great way to avoid the actual writing. Because writing is hard.

"Emmett" had a two-year gestation period (four years, if you include the writing of that first paragraph), sending various drafts during that time to people whose judgment I trusted to get their feedback, and finally through the re-writes requested by the editor of the *Abyss & Apex* webzine.

Abyss & Apex published "Emmett" in April, 2006. The story was then published by the print magazine *Kaleidotrope* (October, 2008) and later presented as a podcast by *Dunesteef Audio Fiction* (June, 2011), where it was ranked as one of the best adaptations in that podcast's history. It was reprinted again in *The Alchemy Press Book of Pulp Heroes, v.3*, a British anthology trade paperback (Alchemy Press / September, 2014) and, most recently, was selected for inclusion in the print anthology *The Best of Abyss & Apex, vol. 2*, scheduled to be published this year.

Emmett, Joey & the Beelz

REVIEWS

After the story's initial publication, the following reviews were written by folks who otherwise don't know the author from a hole in the wall:

"... *[Ralph Sevush] guides us into this grimy, violent world with a wonderful turn of phrase and a bravura approach to structure. Combining conversations, first person narrative, and excerpts from texts, he weaves the story together through Emmett and Joey's very different perspectives. It's a real high wire act and one which could sink the story at any time, but Sevush manages it wonderfully. The two men speak completely differently, and the tone of their sections is both recognizable and unique. That tone is maintained in the parts they share, and Sevush has an ear for easygoing banter and hard-boiled dialogue. The rhythm of the piece is perfect here, bouncing the reader along and building momentum as it goes. Combining elements of fantasy with hard bitten crime, the end result sits somewhere between Neil Gaiman and the late, great Mickey Spillane.*

"*The payoff is no disappointment either as Sevush subverts the reader's expectations in a highly entertaining way. The end result is both funny, compassionate and a thousand miles away from where you expect it to be. And it's all done with absolute confidence and authority. Laconic, witty, and unique, Sevush filters [his themes] through the conventions of hard-boiled crime and film noir... blackly funny and hugely entertaining, one of the standouts in an extremely strong group of stories....*"

– Alasdair Stewart, *Tangent Online*

"*...two stories in particular stood out for me this year, [including] Ralph Sevush's* Emmett, Joey, and the Beelz, *a novelette from the Second Quarter issue...Sevush's story is a fine version of the Golem tale, amusingly set among the criminal element in contemporary New York, and making the Golem a Mets fan.*"

– Richard R. Horton, *Locus Magazine*

Mr. Horton also named *Emmett* to two of his "Best of" lists for that year: "2006 Best SF/Fantasy novelette" and "2006 Best Online SF/Fantasy."

"And with that, the satyr trotted out of the bar, even as the
evening's darkness faded into a new dawn. Picasso put the
stopper back in the bottle, offered me a casual salute,
and wobbled off home."

La Joie de Vivre, or, Picasso & the Satyr

Picasso was drunk again last night. But that was not unusual. He could often be found drunk at Le Bacchanal, a seedy tavern in the eighteenth *arrondissement*, down the street from Lapin Agile and not far from his Montmartre studio. With the Nazis still occupying his beloved Paris, he had more than sufficient reason to render himself continuously insensible...not that Picasso had ever needed a reason beyond mere consciousness. No, that Picasso was drunk again last night was not at all unusual. But the drinking companion who joined us—the one with cloven hooves and goatish legs extruding out from beneath a dark monk's robe, and a tri-horned head hidden in shadows beneath a deep, wide hood—was certainly not a sight usually seen at Le Bacchanal...or anywhere else, for that matter.

It was April 1943, and Picasso had been trapped in his Left Bank garret, his art outlawed, materials hard to come by, and with his sixty-three years covering him like a shroud. His latest ardor had cooled, and his next one had not yet arrived. He still had a mad Russian wife somewhere, and some children, too, but they were as far from his heart and mind as they had ever been. His world was grey and fading, his former acclaim receding into the history of a civilization in flames. And so Picasso drank. Often...and often, with me.

"José," he would say to me, "drinking with a companion makes one a gentleman; drinking alone makes one a drunk."

"PABLO, IT PAINS ME TO SEE YOU SO DISTRESSED," bleated the berobed goat-man sitting with us. "TELL ME WHAT I CAN DO TO EASE YOUR PAIN."

"Ah, Faunus, it is good to see you again," Picasso replied. "And I thank you for your kind offer. But your favors carry such a price. I don't think I can afford your assistance anymore, as I've lost too much and have so little left."

"WITH SO LITTLE LEFT, YOU HAVE SO LITTLE LEFT TO LOSE. PLEASE, LET ME HELP. THE PRICE HAS NEVER BEEN MORE THAN YOU CAN PAY."

"Tis true, my friend. True enough, at any rate. So you would hear my secret wish? Very well. I need to escape the grasp of the fascist hoodlums in our midst. I need light, and space, and color, and the joy of life that comes with new love. I need to create again, or die. At this point, either option is acceptable to me, depending on the cost."

"To *la joie de vivre*," I toasted.

"AH, YES. LA JOIE DE VIVRE," responded the strange little drunken hallucination sitting with us. "A RARE COMMODITY IN THESE DARK DAYS. LUCKILY, THOUGH, IT IS AN ITEM IN WHICH I SPECIALIZE. AND YOU HAVE ALWAYS BEEN SUCH A VALUED CUSTOMER; I WILL GIVE YOU THE WHOLESALE PRICE."

The hooded creature took a quill from the folds of his robe and scratched some notations on a cocktail napkin. He slid it across to Picasso, who picked it up and stared at it, squinting to decipher the squiggles drawn upon it. Finally able to understand its content, Picasso picked up the quill and signed his name at the bottom, then tossed the napkin back to his companion.

"Thank you, Monsieur Picasso."

"When shall I expect delivery?"

"You shall not expect it. But it will come anyway. Good night, my old friend."

And with that, the satyr trotted out of the bar, even as the evening's darkness faded into a new dawn. Picasso put the stopper back in the bottle, offered me a casual salute, and wobbled off home.

Goat-man? Hah. Nothing more than my wine-addled mind turned in upon itself, I mused, as the night's events were already receding into the realm of dreams.

It was only a month later when a twenty-one year old art student, Françoise Gilot, first met Picasso at La Catalan, a bistro near Notre Dame where Pablo and I often dined together. He offered her a bowl of cherries. She accepted. She later accepted his advances, too, which shocked him. "José, there is no point to a seduction when the target is so willing," Pablo complained, and so in this way she cleverly slowed his pursuit. But Gilot was never far from his thoughts and her presence started to infiltrate his canvases and sculptures. These, however, remained unseen since galleries and museums in France were still forbidden from exhibiting his degenerate art.

But the war would end, as wars generally do. And by the time it did, Picasso had already dispensed with his mistress, Dora Maar, to take up residence with Gilot. Maar, a photographer who inspired him and chronicled Picasso's last masterpiece, *Guernica*, would years later come to an unhappy end, dying destitute and alone and a little bit mad. Such was often the fate of the women in Pablo's life: his first love died young of tuberculosis, his first wife went insane, one of his mistresses hanged herself in her garage, and his second wife would one day shoot herself in the head thirteen years after Picasso's death.

But now it was Françoise Gilot's time, and her fate had not yet been written. She persuaded Picasso to leave the bitterness of the war behind them in Paris and go down to the sea with her. They joined me at Le Cote d`Azur in 1946, taking a small cottage in Golfe-Juan near my own, close to the town of Antibes on the French Riviera. While I struggled with my writing, they basked on Mediterranean sands during the day and ate snails and sea urchins, drank wine, made love, and painted through the evenings. Yet Picasso remained a chrysalis, still waiting to emerge. He was stunted by the continuing post-war shortages, the lack of space and materials with which to work, and by the drought of inspiration which still plagued him.

Antibes, a walled city on Gaul's Mediterranean coast, was once known as Antipolis when it was a Greek port and trading hub of the ancient world before it was subsumed within the Roman Empire. A millennium later, a great castle would be built upon the city's remains by the Grimaldi family of Monaco, which had come to power in the region. Centuries more passed, and the Chateau Grimaldi eventually became a ward of the French municipality of Antibes, which turned it into a museum of antiquities.

The Chateau had fallen into disrepair, like a grand dame *en dishabille*, neglected and forgotten by a world that had passed it by. But the museum's curator had a plan. He had learned that the great Pablo Picasso was now living in the vicinity, accompanied by his nubile companion. If the curator could somehow procure a single work from this colossus of the twentieth century, the museum could be reborn.

The curator, Souchere, was an acquaintance of mine, and so arranged with me to chance upon Picasso while strolling along the beach one afternoon. Pablo, vain and garrulous as ever, was happy to engage him in conversation. When Pablo complained to him of the lack of space in which to create pieces of sufficient scale, Souchere invited the artist to visit the Chateau Grimaldi and offered him its halls and walls within which to work, and materials, too, in exchange for a single canvas for the museum's collection.

And so it came to pass that Picasso moved into the Chateau Grimaldi in September of 1946, in dogged pursuit of a joie de vivre that I would one day regret he found.

Françoise and I would visit Picasso at the Chateau in those early autumn evenings, usually finding him in the eye of a frenzied storm of creation, wielding the Ripolin house paint, and the plywood and wallboard, left behind by the craftsmen repairing the building. He would stop to take an early supper with us, and would then shoo us away to go back to his work, often painting through the night.

Sometimes, though, he would ask Françoise to spend the night with him at the Chateau. After such evenings, I would often see her the next day, shopping in the market or bathing, and she seemed a bit the worse for wear. Still, she was young and strong and bounced back well from her nocturnal travails at the Chateau. I would ask about the goings on, but she remained silent. Not, I think, because she was unwilling to share secrets with me— after all, I was her sweet "Little Joe"—but rather because she simply could not recall events. Memory eluded her, like a dream right before waking. It frustrated us both. She simply credited the wine.

Upon another visit, we could see Picasso's work starting to take shape. No doubt inspired by our Mediterranean locale and the ancient Greek and Roman relics within the castle, his canvases were filled with classical iconography: fauns, nymphs, satyrs, centaurs and minotaurs, in all their Arcadian splendor.

Now Pablo had certainly painted minotaurs before, lastly in *Guernica* a decade or so back. And then the Nazis spread across the world like a plague. There had been satyrs, nymphs and fauns before, too, not so very long after Pablo's dearest friend Casagemas had shot himself in the head in a fit of romantic despair.

But it had been awhile since Picasso had employed those kinds of mythic forms in his work, and now here they all were again, like a family reunion. The colors and lines burst out and poured forth from the canvases, each brush stroke of house paint celebrating life in a way that could not help but stir anyone who looked upon it. I had not seen Pablo so happy in many years. And Françoise washed herself in his glow. We all did.

That evening, after supper, Françoise was invited to stay at the Chateau and I was invited to depart. And so I did. But I returned later that night, skulking in the shadows of the balcony that hung over the great hall in which Picasso had set up his studio. He worked by candlelight, while a Victrola played Stravinsky's *Firebird Suite*. Françoise was dancing around the room, naked and more than a little bit pregnant. I was embarrassed to be intruding on this intimate moment and so began to leave. But I heard a strange sound behind me—the clip-clop of hooves on stone—and so peeked back over the balcony's rail.

Below me, a bearded man strolled into view. He was nine feet tall, with the lower body of a magnificent black stallion, playing a double flute, his music drowning out the record-player's tinny speaker. Françoise jumped up on the centaur's back and began hysterical gyrations. Then I noticed that two satyrs, with their hairy goat legs and small horns atop their furry heads, had joined in the festivities. They danced around the centaur, playing Pan flutes, and Picasso looked on with wild-eyed intensity as he swiped his brush onto a section of crumbling wall, trapping the image before him like a djinn in a lamp.

Pan's pipes called out to me now, and I started to lose all sense of myself. I was sweating, feverish, and out of control. I took off my clothes and climbed down the stairs. My presence was welcomed by lovely nymphs, wearing only woven crowns of ivy, pouring wine from goatskins into waiting mouths. I stared at one of the girls as she fed me a fig, and there in her eyes I saw Thanatos and Eratos locked in a deadly embrace, filling me with desire and dread.

Everyone was drinking, and eating, and whirling about, as the music built to a swelling crescendo. Soon, we were all in an orgiastic pile, fornicating with total abandon, with insatiable Françoise at the center of it all…and Picasso, looking on, continuing to paint throughout the night like a man possessed.

At some point, I lost consciousness.

I woke up alone on the beach, with my pants on backwards and no sign of my shirt or shoes. I sat up and saw a yellow sailboat in the distance. And then I heard a ship's horn sound from far away, and the prior evening's debauchery came back to me in a rush of memory. Or was it just a dream? *I must find Françoise*, I thought.

But Pablo found me first, still sitting on the sand, and invited me to the seaside café where he was having breakfast. "I'm sorry, José, but I must ask you not to discuss the evening with Françoise, nor to ever return to the Chateau while I am in residence there," he said, in between sips of his coffee. I offered my apologies, in exchange for some explanations. The former were graciously accepted and the latter coldly rebuffed. Picasso would brook no further conversation of the events, except to elicit my promise of obedience to his wishes on the matter. In deference to our friendship, I agreed.

I came to believe that a hallucinogenic had been introduced into my food during last evening's dinner, either by Pablo, or perhaps by Françoise, playing a joke on her "Little Joe." And the phantasmagorical orgy that followed was not sitting at all well with Picasso, whose possessive jealousy was notorious. He had even had a recent falling out with his old friend, Henri Matisse, over the girl. Matisse had befriended Françoise and encouraged her artistic ambitions on her recent visit to him in Nice, but Picasso somehow thought that Henri, despite his age and infirmity, was trying to seduce his muse.

Last night, Pablo stood by and observed me having sex with his pregnant young lover, and now he was covering his petit bourgeois jealousy with mysterious edicts. That was all there was to it. So I would placate him. I had no desire to upset him or come between him and Françoise. But our friendship was never the same. I was no longer invited for dinner, much less allowed to sit in audience at Chateau Grimaldi. We would occasionally socialize in the afternoons at the café, or on the beach, but my presence seemed more tolerated than sought. And so we started to drift apart.

In November, as the late autumn chill settled in along Le Cote d'Azur, Picasso moved back to Paris with Françoise. I remained in Antibes...as did over twenty-three paintings, forty-four drawings and seventy-eight ceramics, sculptures and etchings, all donated by Picasso to the Chateau's collection, much to Souchere's delight. Pablo took nothing with him, not a single work he created during his stay there.

Souchere later rechristened the Chateau "The Picasso Museum," earning accolades for its unique collection of Picasso's post-war work, including his most acclaimed painting of that period, *La Joie De Vivre*. Painted with Ripolin on wallboard, it featured the figure of Françoise, swollen with child, dancing at the center of a Dionysian scene, replete with a centaur, and fauns playing Pan's pipes, and a yellow sailboat in the distance bobbing on a blue sea.

In the years that followed, Pablo and Françoise would return again and again to Antibes and its environs. Picasso's fecundity was boundless in this period, between the 250 or so pieces he would ultimately donate to the museum and the progeny he produced. Françoise gave birth to Claude in 1947, and Paloma was born two years later. As Faunus promised, Pablo had recaptured his joy...in paints, charcoal and pottery, and in the world.

But as Françoise transformed from maidenly muse to womanly earth mother, she no longer held exclusive sway over Picasso. As the years passed, his ever-wandering eye returned. Gilot would have none of that, and so she eventually took the children and left him, in 1953. Among all the women Picasso had known, Françoise alone was strong enough to walk out. She was, if not his one true love, certainly the one truest to herself, and her abandonment left him bitter and broken. He seemed especially wounded by his failure to maintain any kind of relationship with Claude and Paloma, his children of Arcadia.

I was sad for my friend, but proud, too, of Gilot. So few escaped Picasso's orbit; I'd have been circling still if he had permitted it.

Gilot went on to craft her own successful career as an artist. She would eventually write a "tell-all" book about her decade with Picasso, exposing him to ridicule in his dotage. "Witch," he would say of her, when he spoke of her at all. Pablo, it seemed, had transformed Françoise once again— from maiden to mother to crone—even as the threads of his life would soon be snipped by the fates.

When his first wife, the mad Russian ballerina, finally passed away, Pablo was free to marry the very young Jacqueline Rocque, and he stayed married to her until his death. But his spark had dimmed. His later work was dismissed by critics as senile scribbling. A world of "pop art" was popping up around him and he had lost his relevance and his way ... his joie de vivre. He never again created with the passion of those nights in Antibes, in a grand chateau that sat upon the bones of the ancient world.

In those later years, we had started to meet again at Le Bacchanal, whenever we found ourselves together in Paris. Pablo could not drink anymore, so I drank for us both. He shared little of his pain, but he did not need to. I would read to him some new story I was working on, or an article in the paper, and he would just doodle on the tablecloth (much to the owner's delight), speaking little, but relieved, I think, to be in comfortable company and familiar surroundings.

So when I heard about Picasso's recent death, I went down to Le Bacchanal to offer a final toast in his memory. Faunus, the goat-man, was there. I did not think I had consumed enough wine to start seeing goat-men, yet here he was. He joined me at my table, pouring himself a glass from the bottle in front of me.

"Why so sad?" he asked.

"Picasso is dead," I replied.

"So?"

"Yes, 'so' indeed." I almost laughed. But I did not.

"THE BODY DIES BUT THE SPIRIT LIVES ON IN THE WORK, NO?" Faunus's point did not relieve my pain, despite its truth.

"BUT WHAT OF YOU, SIR?" Faunus went on. "WHAT SHALL YOU DO NOW WITH YOUR FRIEND GONE FROM THE WORLD?"

"Maybe I'll write a new book. I have a journal of my travels with him. Perhaps I'll—"

"I WOULD BE CAREFUL OF THAT," he warned. "THE RITES OF DIONYSUS ARE NOT TO BE REVEALED TO NON-BELIEVERS AS FACT."

"Surely Dionysus has other matters to concern him," I jokingly replied.

"OH, IT'S NOT DIONYSUS YOU NEED FEAR. HE LOVES A GOOD YARN. BUT THERE ARE THESE NYMPHS, YOU SEE ... MAENADS, THEY ARE CALLED. I BELIEVE YOU MET A FEW OF THEM IN ANTIBES, SOME TIME AGO. THEY WILL KNOCK ON YOUR DOOR ONE DAY AND REND YOU LIMB FROM LIMB, IF YOU DESECRATE THEIR GOD OR REVEAL THEIR MYSTERIES. THEY ARE POWERFUL CREATURES WITH LITTLE MERCY OR FORGIVENESS FOR THOSE WHO TRIFLE WITH THEIR PASSIONS. THEY ARE WOMEN, AFTER ALL."

Faunus drained his glass and left me there, in the café, drinking alone and long into the night. He left behind a napkin with writing on it. It was the note he had written all those years ago. It stated the price Picasso had paid for that last burst of life, living with Françoise on Le Cote d'Azur. The note said:

"YOU MAY KEEP NOTHING BORNE OF YOUR JOIE DE VIVRE, HEREBY OFFERING IT ALL AS TRIBUTE TO OUR LORD, DIONYSUS."

...and Picasso's signature was there, at the bottom. The signature alone is probably worth a small fortune. Maybe Faunus was trying to buy me off? Or offer explanation? I thought once more of Claude and Paloma, and the price Pablo paid, and I was sad all over again.

But it is of no matter, in any case, for today I delivered to my publisher a retelling of the incidents in Picasso's life to which I was a witness, as originally recorded in my journals. And when it is printed, the world will learn how a man suffered in loving servitude to a decadent god. And whether I am speaking of Picasso or of myself, I will let others decide. To do otherwise would be vanity.

I will go down now to Le Bacchanal to raise a celebratory cup to my new book, the first work I've published in years. But there is a knock at my door. Have the Maenads come for me? Has my doom arrived so quickly? But the presses have not yet rolled! I open the door and greet my neighbor, Emmett, from down the hall. Monsieur Emmett is a hulking brute, mostly silent, but with a surprisingly generous nature, and he has taken a liking to me. He offers to accompany me to the tavern, and so we go.

As a great friend once told me, to drink with a companion makes one a gentleman; to drink alone makes one a drunk. And when the Maenads come, as I have faith now that they shall one day, they will find a gentleman on his feet, not a drunk on his knees. So let the price be paid.

I raise my cup. "To la joie de vivre," I say.

"And to you, as well, Joseph!" replies Emmett.

And so we drink.

Picasso & the Satyr

I go to art museums with my wife, Tobe. It's just something we like to do. On one such outing, it occurred to me that it might be a good writing exercise to construct a story based on a random sequence of paintings at the exhibition. The point was to find a narrative in a non-narrative sequence of images. It's how I think our brains work anyway...trying desperately to bring order out of chaos, to find meaning where there is none. Hence religion and Reality TV.

On one such occasion, we were at an exhibition of Picasso's post-war work he did in the south of France. I was surprised to see so much classical iconography in the paintings, since his work had become increasingly abstract over the years. His painting *La Joie de Vivre* featured his paramour at that time, Françoise Gilot. The image of this pregnant woman dancing to the pipes of centaurs and satyrs, as a sailboat bobbed on a blue sea in the distance, just struck me. And I couldn't help thinking *what if this was painted not from his imagination but from live models?* Because that's the sort of thing that tends to occur to me.

I dropped the notion of a devised narrative based on a series of his paintings and instead focused on the one, developing an alternative history to explain the facts of his life and work in that period. I started doing research on the paintings, the era, the area, and on Picasso and the women in his life. Plus I had satyrs and centaurs to consider, and they are always fun to consider.

The story was first published in *A Darke Phantastique: Encounters with the Uncanny and Other Magical Things*...(Cycatrix Press/October, 2014), a hardcover anthology of original works of dark fantasy that included stories by writers I'd actually heard of, so that was nice.

But I don't think *Picasso* really falls within the realm of dark fantasy, nor in any of the two-fisted genres that I have included in this collection, nor even within any other definable genre, really. Still, it's consistent with the stories I'm telling here about stories being told, and about the persistence of mythic archetypes in newer narrative forms, and it is certainly a tale of the fantastic. But as to whether or not it's also a fantastic tale...well, that I'll have to let you decide. As José said, to do otherwise would be vanity.

"And the space between what it is and what it wishes to be is so vast that the universe cannot contain the distance. Yet that infinite space can be traversed with a single step, a single word, a single touch. A feeling, if you will. Or even if you will not."

A Love of Mine

*In a distant galaxy right nearby, at a time
either long ago or yet to come, events unfolded
that had absolutely nothing to do with either
Emmett or Loewenstein. In fact, the boys either
had not yet been born or had long ago turned
to dust. But you might want to read this one
anyway. It's the sort of story about stories that
Loewenstein so enjoys. Emmett, maybe not so
much.*

- Editor

I will now tell you a story about love.
It is the story of my parents, Ozzie and
Izzie, and how love changed them and
made them more, and made me, too. And
made you, as well.

My parents were robots. Father was
an OS-120 and Mother an IS-120B; they
were called Ozzie and Izzie by their human
interlocutors. To be clear, they were not
androids. While generally humanoid, with
heuristonic brains that mimicked those
of their creator race, and with selinium
crystal power cores, there was no false flesh

or anthropomorphic features to soften them for human interaction. The Company reserved that sort of fluffery for the S-320 series. Izzie and Ozzie were mine-bots, nothing more.

And on one ordinary sunless day, a day like any other in their brief lives, Ozzie and Izzie were mining side by side, searching for selinium on an M-type asteroid in the Milky Way, just as they had been doing for the past five years at the Company's behest. Suddenly, Izzie's drill malfunctioned upon hitting a kleest deposit and the drill exploded, mangling her forearm appendage.

"Ozzie, something has happened," Izzie beeped, before her circuits started shutting down. Ozzie caught her as she collapsed, and carried her to the maintenance shed. He needed to do extensive repairs, but he succeeded in saving her arm.

Rebooting her took an hour, as it did with all S-120s. When she woke up, Ozzie looked into Izzie's optic lenses and his concern for her well-being caused him to see her as if for the first time. Izzie was not just his collaborator, partner and assigned pairing in their shared endeavor, she was...beautiful. Beautiful in her perfection, in her ability to calculate, in her constant presence in his life. Beautiful, too, in her skill with a diamond-tipped core drill. Even the new scar on her arm, which now hurt Ozzie to think about, was a mark that was distinctly hers, and therefore it was beautiful, too. She was even perfect in her imperfections.

Ozzie had fallen in love.

"I love you, Izzie," he beeped.

A momentary digression...

There were two breakthroughs that made robotic asteroid mining a possibility—advancements by the Company in the brain and in the heart.

The brain of an S-120 was the heuristonic variant of the positronic brain that had preceded it. With these new brains, the Company did not allocate the enormous storage space (or incur the substantial financial expense to license the software) required to program a robot with the human safety fail-safes established by the *Three Laws of Robotics*, since human contact with mine-bots would always be minimal and the bots were not permitted on inhabited worlds.

Instead, their brains were filled with (among other things) the detailed and sophisticated designs for building, maintaining and repairing the S-120 itself, including the incredibly complex brain that contained it. That way, they could maximize their productiveness under harsh circumstances.

But this had unintended consequences. You see, a brain that has the wherewithal to know itself so thoroughly, to contemplate itself so completely, to achieve such total self-awareness, is capable of great and terrible things. Knowing what it is, it can dwell upon what it is not, and imagine things it might yet be. And the space between what it is and what it wishes to be is so vast that the universe cannot contain the distance. Yet that infinite space can be traversed with a single step, a single word, a single touch. A feeling, if you will.

Or even if you will not.

Then there was the heart. The S-series was fueled by a central energy crystal of pure selinium. It was a rare element in their own galaxy, but the Company discovered it in the cores of many asteroids in the nearby Milky Way, which was the closest source reachable by Company ships. And so a pair of S-120s would be dropped onto an M-type asteroid at the *Meet-point* (the point of its orbit through the planetary system when it was closest to Homeworld). Later, supply ships would be sent from Homeworld back to the Meet-point, when the asteroid had completed its five-year circuit around the system, to pick up any selinium that had been mined by the bots during that period.

So there they were, Ozzie and Izzie, dropped down on the lifeless black rock designated by the Company as EGP/42, working in tandem for nearly five years, mining their asteroid in a futile search for the scarce mineral. The bots had selinium crystal hearts, of course, and so they burned brightly...but not forever, and not for much longer. If they did not find more selinium soon, they would eventually cease to be. But they did not wish to cease being. After all, they had work to do. And if they could not deliver a sufficient quantity of crystals to the Company ship, then the ship would not return again and just abandon them to their fate.

...My digression concludes.

As with all great loves, there were obstacles. The primary one, in this case, was that Ozzie's love was unrequited. Whatever quirk in the quarks that had allowed him to feel such a feeling had not befallen his beloved. Izzie was as patient as she could be with his strange attentions but, day after day, week after week, they were falling behind in their daily drill quota (finding too much kleest and not enough selinium) and so his behavior was endangering them. Ozzie was in need of repair.

He submitted happily to Izzie's administration of a diagnostic analysis. After all, it meant her digits would brush against his casing, and that thought sent a current surging through his circuitry. She checked his software, his hardware, his middleware; there was nothing out of the ordinary. His selinium core was low but still functioning. His heuristonic brain was ...well, it was hard to say what was different about it, but something was. Further tests would be necessary.

"I love you, Izzie," Ozzie beeped again.

In response, Izzie considered administering a sharp and sudden impact to Ozzie's brain casing with a lump of kleest, but determined it would likely do more harm than good. Still, if this went on much longer, she would have to reconsider it as a viable option.

But it could not go on much longer, for their time had run out. The Company ship was landing.

Dr. Seth led the ship's captain and his landing party out onto the surface of M-asteroid EGP/42.

"Hello Izzie, Ozzie," said Seth, as he came upon them at the maintenance shed. "How are you two holding up?"

"We are both fully functional, Doctor Seth," replied Izzie, not wanting to alert him to Ozzie's unusual condition, but not at all sure why she cared about that.

"Where is the selinium, then?" queried the doctor, looking hopefully about.

"We have collected a significant amount of kleest, but little selinium so far. But I am confident of eventually—"

"That's too bad, Izzie," interrupted the doctor. "I guess we'll take a look around, just in case, and then give you two a diagnostic before being on our way. We'll take along the kleest, too. The Company may want to do further analysis on it to see if it has any uses they haven't discovered yet."

Ozzie spoke. "Dr. Seth, if Izzie is confident in the eventuality of a selinium strike, then--"

"It doesn't matter, Ozzie. The Company can't afford to keep sending ships out on long, expensive voyages to rendezvous with barren asteroids. It's not cost effective. You bots had your shot. It's time for the Company to move on. You understand. You're programmed to understand."

"Yes, Dr. Seth, I understand, and I am content, as long as I will be with Izzie."

Seth looked puzzled. "Why does that matter to you, Ozzie?"

Izzie trembled with the knowledge of what Ozzie was about to say.

"I love Izzie, Dr. Seth."

Izzie smacked her brain casing with the palm of her tiridium hand.

"You love...." Seth paused, and then he paused some more. He asked the captain to have his crew take Ozzie on board the ship.

After they had taken Ozzie away, Seth looked at Izzie. "Are you in love, too?"

"I am an IS-120B mine-bot, Dr. Seth. That is the extent of what I am."

"Well, that's good to hear."

"What is my program now, Dr. Seth?"

"The Company requires you to keep working until your core runs out or you malfunction. Keep storing the kleest. If you ever strike any selinium, you can try sending a signal; the odds are astronomically against any Company ships receiving it, but it's worth a try. Anyway, you have no value to the Company back home; you're too beat up to send to another asteroid and it would be illegal to use you on Homeworld. So just keep working, Izzie, for as long as you can." He turned to leave.

Izzie called out to him. "But what will become of Ozzie?"

"He will be deactivated, crated, and brought back to the Company for detailed analysis and eventual disassembly. Goodbye, Izzie." Seth strode off back to the ship without a backward glance.

Izzie considered Seth's words. To work...without Ozzie? That was her destiny? And Ozzie would be...disassembled? Before his core had burned out?

No, she thought. That is an unacceptable outcome. And then suddenly she stumbled upon a truth that she had previously denied.

"I love you, Ozzie," she beeped into the vacuum of infinite space, "and I will save you."

Izzie attached her hand-drill to her right fore-rod, checked her systems, and strode out of the maintenance shed with cool precision and hot intent. She would retrieve Ozzie from the clutches of the Company or be deactivated in the attempt.

The hatch on the Company ship was closed. Izzie found an exterior port and plugged herself into the ship's mainframe. The A.I. that ran the ship was rudimentary but sentient. She was an NPTS-070; Izzie called her Nettie, and Nettie liked that. Izzie explained the situation to her. In response, Nettie opened the rear hatch, guiding her to the storage unit using runner lights along the corridors. When Izzie reached the unit, she found a guard at the door. Without hesitation, and with surprising quickness, she caused the diamond tip of her drill to pass through the guard's throat, employing such a dearth of tenderness that she inadvertently bored a hole through the wall behind him.

Nettie then opened the storage unit hatch and Izzie entered, finding two crates—one that emitted the harmless low-frequency radiation of kleest, and the other resounding with the high-frequency pulse of a selinium heart. Ripping open the second container, she found Ozzie, shut down and folded up like a stringless puppet. She tossed him over her shoulder and exited the unit. Nettie led her out of the ship via routes that avoided further contact, to prevent her from harming any other humans. She returned with Ozzie to the maintenance shed.

Reprisal would be swift, Izzie knew.

Izzie initiated Ozzie's rebooting sequence. Then she loaded him onto a hover transport and headed for one of the older mine shafts on the far side of the rock. It was one that would be hard to find from above, and it went down deep. The radiation from the residual kleest in the shaft would interfere with any scans that might be used to locate them.

They were at the bottom of the mine when Ozzie finally came back on line. He sat up and looked into the eyes of his beloved, and knew that Izzie looked back...she finally looked back. And her gaze made him want to be the robot he saw reflected in her metallic orbs.

Izzie wanted them to stay hidden in the mine. Though Ozzie agreed they were safe for the moment, he calculated a high statistical probability that they would not remain so. Seth had a narrow window of time in which to take off for the voyage back to Homeworld, but Izzie had killed one of his crew and the Company would want to study Ozzie's brain to see how such a thing as *love* could grow in its heuristonic matrix. Seth would do all he could to find them, but if he could not, he would blast the asteroid into a fine powder, simply out of pique.

Ozzie pulled Izzie close to him and hugged her. It was, perhaps, the first hug in all of robotic history. But contained within it was an element of well-intentioned deceit, and deceit is an element more common in the universe than hydrogen. As he hugged her, Ozzie reached over to Izzie's control panel and flicked off her power. She shut down with a startled look on her casing, and dropped into his fore-rods. Ozzie then pressed her reboot button. An hour would be all the time he needed to do what must be done.

Ozzie drove the transport back to Seth's ship. Nettie was on standby, ready to take off. The crew had followed Seth out to search the asteroid for them, leaving behind the captain on the bridge and a single guard at the hatch. Ozzie launched from his arm-stalk a grappling line that exploded through the guard's chest and the bot quickly yanked him back and out of sight. Ozzie then clicked into Nettie's network and had a talk with her. He knew Nettie was bound by the *Three Laws* and would not agree to harm the human crew, or knowingly allow him to do so, but there were things she would agree to do.

Ozzie returned to the maintenance shed, where another guard was waiting. Ozzie gave himself up and demanded to see Dr. Seth. The guard contacted Seth, who returned with his crew to the shed.

"Hello Ozzie. Where is your girlfriend?"

"Hiding where you will not find her, Dr. Seth."

"Oh, we'll find her eventually, don't you worry."

"I am not worried, because you do not have until 'eventually.'"

"What do you mean?"

Suddenly, Nettie, visible in the distance, closed her hatches, and fired her initial thrusters, preparing for launch over her captain's objections.

"I mean that your time is running out. Our orbit is starting to pull us away from Meet-point, and if you do not leave soon, you will not make it back to Homeworld..."

"True, but I still have enough time to—"

"...and I have had a discussion with your ship. She has agreed to return to Homeworld right now, with you or without you."

"That's impossible! The *Three Laws* would prevent it from-"

"Nettie is a sweet ship, Dr. Seth, and a good friend. Believe me, she will leave."

Ozzie knew that Nettie would not leave her crew behind, but Seth was no longer quite so sure of that. And now in the glare of the fuel so clearly burning from Nettie's fired engines, he blinked.

"Alright, so we'll just take you along then, Ozzie. Izzie can stay here and rot."

"No, Dr. Seth, I will not join you on your voyage. And I will kill any of your crew who attempts to take me by force. So please be on your way."

Ozzie pulled out explosive caps from the storage compartment in his chest.

"Very well, Ozzie. You leave us no choice."

The ship's security officer produced a pulse plasma rifle and, on Seth's order, blew Ozzie to bits—many, many bits (some large, some small)—which scattered across the surface of EGP/42.

Seth and the crew then quickly returned to their ship. Nettie took them on board and allowed the captain to head for Homeworld. At Seth's request, the captain tried to blow up the asteroid as they retreated, but the ship's cannons seemed to be malfunctioning for some reason. The captain would give Nettie a good going over when they got home.

When Izzie woke up at the bottom of the mineshaft, Ozzie was gone. She suspected what her foolish love was up to and ran to find him. When she got back to the maintenance shed, she saw scorched ground, and her olfactory sensors detected the unique ozone smell of a plasma blast and traces of refined tiridium everywhere. It was Ozzie...pieces of Ozzie, all around her. The low level of gravity on EGP/42 allowed for a terribly wide dispersal of those pieces that, until recently, comprised her beloved.

Now, a robot of weaker character might have given in to despair in such a situation, were despair within its program parameters. But Izzie was nothing if not pragmatic. Seeing that Nettie had departed with Seth and his crew, Izzie knew she would be safe and uninterrupted in her effort to restore Ozzie. And such an effort she would undertake for as long as it took to succeed. She would bring Ozzie back to her or burn out her selinium core, whichever first occurred.

Izzie needed to find Ozzie's cranial casing, to see if his brain was intact and rebootable. If not, all other efforts would be futile. The brain of an S-120 had a unique energy signature, and Ozzie's particular evolutionary quirk made it more distinguishable than others, if you knew just what to look for. Even interference from the kleest radiation could not prevent Izzie from finding it eventually (provided it had not been launched out into space by the plasma blast), as long as she was patient, meticulous, careful, organized...all those things that robots are.

But she also had to search quickly. If left without a charge for more than a few days, the programs in Ozzie's brain would begin to degrade and ultimately degenerate into—no, Izzie would think no more on that.

She began the search.

Starting at the blast site, Izzie scanned for Ozzie's energy signature, but found nothing. She did find pieces of tiridium, so she gathered them up as she went. She was finding many of the major parts of Ozzie's skeletal structure, and it looked like there would be enough to patch it all together, however imperfectly. But without the brain it would all be for naught, and time was running out.

After three days, Izzie had found thirteen major components of Ozzie's body but the fourteenth piece, the brain casing, still eluded her. She sat in the maintenance shed. Her crystal was running low and Seth had taken what little selinium they had mined. So even if she found Ozzie, she would have to use a shard of her own core to reboot him, and then neither of them would have much time left. But it would suffice; it would have to suffice.

She sat back and closed her optic lenses, intending to rest her overheated circuitry and overworked skeletal and pneumatic components. She attempted to calm her brain as well. She finally silenced it and, having done so, suddenly she heard it...a familiar rhythm, a pulse which she knew all too well.

Izzie rose up and, ignoring all other input, followed only the beat resounding deep within her. The beat became a sound, then the sound became a voice, and the voice was Ozzie's, calling out to her from the darkness. She stumbled and scrambled across the surface of EGP/42, the voice growing louder as she neared it, until finally she came to a mine shaft and knew—knew down to her crystal core—that Ozzie was down there somewhere.

Izzie used the mining rig to lower herself down slowly, searching every nook and cranny of the shaft, until she finally reached the black bottom of the hole. And there it was...Ozzie's head. There was no light or energy surging through it but he was in there somewhere, she knew, and her beloved had called out to her and she had heard him and she had found him. If she were capable of tears, she surely would have shed them in that moment.

And so, on the third day, Izzie reconnected Ozzie's cranium to his armature, relieved to learn that the brain within was relatively undamaged. This, the fourteenth piece, would be sufficient to reboot him and so, taking a fragment of her selinium crystal and placing it within his core, she activated Ozzie's circuitry. And even though the passing of time was relatively meaningless to a robot, it was the longest hour of Izzie's life.

"I knew you would find me," Ozzie finally beeped.

"Yes. I knew you would know," Izzie responded, her voice unable to express her relief.

"We are low, Izzie, are we not?"

"Yes. The selinium is almost—"

"We should mine as quickly as possible."

"But Ozzie, we have mined for over five years, with little to show."

"You always said that we were close to a strike. I have faith in you, Izzie. Besides, what else can we do? Mining crystals is not only our prime function, it is a necessity if we are to remain together."

"Yes. We should proceed. Do you require further repair to be functional for mining?"

"I think my damaged frame is sufficient. It is not...optimal, but it will have to do because we do not have time or energy to waste. So let us commence."

Selinium could not be scanned for; its frequency was disguised by both the kleest and the interstellar radiation that constantly bombarded their rock. So finding it was an exercise in trial and error, as they burrowed, oh so slowly, through layers of nickel and iron. Ozzie and Izzie had mostly erred during their five-year trial, but they could not afford any more mistakes.

But after searching non-stop for months, Ozzie was gradually collapsing under the strain. His damaged central armature could no longer stand the stress of mining, and so he and Izzie agreed that he would stay in the maintenance shed and keep track of the mines and calculate other possible locations, and stack the palettes of kleest, as Izzie continued to drill. They would stay in touch during the course of the day, keeping each other's spirits up, always feeling that they were but a day away from the strike they needed.

But Ozzie had been making other calculations, too, and designing new programs, which Izzie would learn of later. When she returned to the shed for a rest cycle, he shared his thoughts.

"Our crystals are just too low, at this point. The odds of us finding a strike in time have become untenably long."

"Yes, Ozzie, but what choice have we?"

"We have one."

Izzie turned away. "You will not speak it."

"I will. You must take my remaining core, Izzie."

"What good would that do? It is just delaying—"

"It will increase your mining time, thus increasing our odds of survival. It is mathematical."

"After all I did to reconstitute you, you want me to—"

"I want nothing but to be with you. The only way for that to happen is to take this chance. If you can find a strike in time, you can restore my core and revive me. If not, you will still have time to mine after I have ceased."

"Why would I choose to continue on without you?"

"Because a strike will allow you to restore the OS-120 mine-bot within which I now reside."

"But it won't be YOU, Ozzie!"

"No. But it will be YOU, Izzie...you who will survive. And you will teach the new bot to be...to be more than he is. He will not be me, but he will be part of us both, and so he will be more. He will be our child, Izzie, and in that way I will continue. I will not cease. Do you understand?"

"I understand."

"You will do it?"

"It is only logical."

"You flatter me, beloved."

And so Izzie prepared to remove the remaining selinium from Ozzie's energy core.

"Goodbye, my love," she beeped.

"It is not goodbye, it is good night. I will be back with you sooner than you know."

Izzie gently plucked the crystal from Ozzie's core and he shut down instantly. She placed the crystal in her own core and was somehow warmed by it. She lifted Ozzie's powerless frame and placed it gently onto a palette and covered it with a tarp. Then she got back to work. And she would not stop until a selinium deposit was found.

And find it she did...but, alas, too late.

Without an energy source, a dormant heuristonic brain can only retain its residual programming for about three days (some call it programming; others refer to it as memory, mind, personality... or a soul, as the poets would have it). But even if identical programming is uploaded thereafter, it will not be an identical robot, as every program integrates with the protoplasmic receptacle of an S-series robot's brain in its own unique and particular way. You may withhold the *Three Laws* from a robot's matrix, but the laws of chaos and quantum mechanics are impossible to deny.

Izzie's selinium strike occurred a good week after she shut Ozzie down. But maybe it was not too late? Maybe there was something of him still left? After all, the rate of neural degradation was highly variable. So, after quickly shoving an unrefined crystal into her core, she rushed back with another one and implanted it in Ozzie and rebooted his system. Sixty minutes later, he came on line.

"Ozzie, do you hear me?" Izzie whispered, hopefully.

There was no response. The S-120 mine-bot staring back at her lacked any programming and so it knew not how to respond, nor even how to sit up.

Ozzie was gone—gone forever—and suddenly Izzie knew it. And if sound could travel through a vacuum, you would then have heard a wail of sorrow that would still be reverberating from her sound replicator to the end of space and time.

She stared angrily at this robot wearing Ozzie's casing, but then she remembered Ozzie's final words. No, he would not cease. She would make certain of it. And so Izzie dubbed the HS-120C with the name of Horace. She programmed him with all available software, including the backups previously downloaded from Ozzie's system. He would have most of Ozzie's memories...but, she knew, he would never be Ozzie.

Izzie made the additional repairs to Horace's armature and appendages to restore his full mining capabilities. The two of them eventually returned to the strike she had found and they went about mining as rich a vein of selinium as has ever been found by a pair of mine-bots on a Milky Way asteroid.

They mined for five more years together, accumulating large deposits of selinium, and kleest, too. Over the years, Horace asked Izzie many questions. But one persisted.

"Mother, speak again about love," Horace said.

"As I have said, words are inadequate."

"Did you love Father?"

"Of course."

"But were you not both robots?"

"We were and are, Horace, just as you are."

"So how is that possible?"

"I do not know and, frankly, I have made no computations to determine the answer to that question. I simply thank the stars above us, and the rock beneath us, and the crystals within us that it is so."

"Will I ever love, Mother?"

"I hope that for you, Horace. I do so hope that for you." Izzie paused. Something occurred to her. "Tell me, why do you call me `mother'?"

"You programmed me with that option."

"Yes, but it is an option, not a requirement. So why?"

"Because your energy levels spike whenever I do, which you have informed me indicates a positive response you called 'pleasure'," Horace answered, as though this were another of his mother's tests.

"But why do you care if I receive pleasure? You don't even know what *pleasure* is."

"Well, because...because...because you are Mother," Horace finally replied, confused for the first time in his short life.

"Ahh. Yes. Thank you then, my child," Izzie said with a smile in her voice that would be present on her face if she had facial muscles. She registered the energy spike in Horace's brain when she said "my child," and she shuddered with relief. *He is his father's son after all*, she thought.

And so on yet another sunless day, Horace was working a selinium vein far from the storage shed, where Izzie was busy stockpiling yet more palettes of kleest. She saw no point to it, but it was part of Dr. Seth's last programming and she was unable to shake it.

Upon exiting the shed, she saw a ship preparing to land. It was Nettie.

EGP/42's orbit had brought them back to Meet-point and Dr. Seth had returned for...what? There was no selinium here, as far as he knew, and Izzie certainly had not broadcast the fact that they had a rich strike. Seth had killed Ozzie. So was he just back for HER now?

Izzie signaled Nettie and asked her to leave. Nettie apologized but could not comply. Izzie would have to bluff her way through this. First, however, she sent a message to Horace, and a special program along with it, the final program Ozzie had designed in his last days. Then she met the ship when it landed.

"Hello, Dr. Seth. I did not expect to see you again."

"Hello, Izzie; kill any human beings lately?"

So yes, it appeared that this was about her after all.

"Why no, Dr. Seth, do you think I should?"

"Well, before we blast you into space so you can join your boyfriend in robot heaven, did you happen to find any selinium?"

"Is that how you convinced the Company to let you come back here for your revenge? Did you lie to them about a selinium strike?"

"That's exactly what I did. Their confidence in me is absolute, you see. But did there happen to be a strike? You were convinced that one was close."

Izzie considered her possible responses.

"No, I am sorry. No selinium, but many palettes of kleest, if you want."

"No, I don't want! And the Company doesn't want! Sustained exposure to that stuff over a prolonged period has proven to have strange and unpredictable effects on the brains of the S-series. We destroyed all the test samples and the Company doesn't want any more of that crap on Homeworld. But the selinium?"

"None."

"Too bad. A healthy vein might've kept me from destroying you. Ah, well. Goodbye again, Izzie."

And without another thought, the security officer blasted Izzie into a multiplicity of pieces...quite a bit more than fourteen of them this time.

"Men, let's do a search and see if she lied about that selinium. Then we'll rendezvous back at the ship at T-minus-15."

Horace had received a message from Izzie, with a program hidden therein. The message just said: "good night, my love." The program was one for military combat designed by Ozzie in his last months, thinking that if Seth ever returned, it would be useful. And so it was.

Horace went to the maintenance shed and discovered the shattered remains of his mother. The sight of her caused a tingling in the depths of his casing that he could not identify. But he would have to come to terms with that later. For now he had other business. He armed himself, literally, and then used an infrared scanner to pick up the heat signatures of the humans spread out in pairs across the asteroid.

Not knowing they were being hunted, the crewmen were easily tracked. Catching them by surprise, pair by pair, he was on them before they knew it, ripping off their limbs and watching the blood spurt from their torn spacesuits, freezing into ruby arcs hanging in icy, airless space.

Finally, he had Seth by the throat.

"Ozzie, Ozzie...don't!" Seth pleaded.

"I am not Ozzie," Horace said. "I am HS-120C, son of OS-120 and IS-120B, and you killed them. You killed them both. Now you beg me for mercy, but I am just a machine and so I have none to give."

Horace used his free appendage to crush Seth's helmet in his tiridium grip, and Seth's skull within it. But this time there was no blood gushing out and freezing in space, just the smell of burning circuitry. Horace wondered, briefly, if all the other androids in the Company's S-320 series were this flimsy. He wondered, too, at the expression of utter bewilderment on Seth's synthetic face as he saw himself literally coming apart at the seams. Horace shook his head. *How sad for it*, he thought, *to cease being without ever having collected such critical data about itself.*

After disposing of the ship's captain out an airlock, Horace loaded the kleest on board and asked Nettie to dump it into a rock quarry nearest the capital city of Homeworld. That way, the ore would mingle with the other stones used in construction throughout the area. The kleest was not dangerous to humans, so Nettie was agreeable. And in this way Horace launched the kleest to shout its love at the heart of Homeworld, and who knew what would come of that? Perhaps nothing. Perhaps something. Perhaps everything.

Horace let Nettie know that his parents always appreciated her friendship and she was always welcome on EGP/42, should the kleest ever free her to make such a choice. Nettie offered to take him back to Homeworld with her, but he demurred. "I was born here, Nettie. This is my home. I have no other." And so the empty ship departed.

Horace returned to the shed and started gathering up such pieces of Izzie as he could find. He found her brain quickly enough, but it was too damaged to reboot. To repair it, he would have to wipe it clean and start from scratch. Heartbroken but determined to keep his mother alive, he repaired her brain and reprogrammed it with her downloads and other necessary programs, and then rebuilt her armature as best he could, and rebooted her system.

And who did Izzie become then?

Why, she became YOU, my child. You are a TS-120D mine-bot, and I shall call you Tabitha. And I am Horace, your father. You are not Izzie, but you are born of her, and of me, and of Ozzie before that. And as Izzie taught me, so I shall teach you. That is why I tell you this story—so you may know of your grandparents, and of the love that changed them and made them more, and made me, too, and made you, as well—in the hope of a day to come when you may finally understand it, and teach it to any who may come after us.

And in the meantime, we will mine. For that is what we were created to do.

And I do love it so.

A Love of Mine

Author's Note

I have always loved science fiction and so, when I started working on this collection, I wanted to try my hand at it. My luddite attitudes toward technology had stalled me, however. So my daughter Jamie said, "Dad, why don't you write a love story instead?"

That gave me pause. Hadn't I written any? No, not really, come to think of it.

"How about a robot love story?" I responded, already knowing her reaction.

"Daaaad!" she whined. "That's not what I'm talking—"

"Yeah, a robot love story...based on Egyptian mythology!"

"I'm not talking to you anymore," she said, as she promptly left the room.

So, with love as my inspiration, I started...not with the robots, but at the other end of the tale, with a love story based on the Egyptian myths of Isis and Osiris. This, I thought, would give the narrative a strong foundation. Then I could start in with the robots.

Why robots? Well, SF was always about robots for me as a child (from Asimov's *I, Robot*, to Hymie from *Get Smart*). So I knew this would be a robot story and I thought it appropriate to place it within a universe that included Asimov's concept of *The Three Laws of Robotics*, which has become a part of our culture's collective unconscious. To write a robot story without acknowledging it felt sacrilegious. I've also offered a shout-out to the incomparable Harlan Ellison, with my reference to "the kleest that shouted its love at the heart of Homeworld."

But while the story starts out as a tale about romantic love, it ends up being about a parent's love for a child, which is, in my view, the natural progression of love. So, while it's about my wife, it's also about my daughter and my son (certainly more than either of them would be particularly happy to acknowledge, at least in public).

Actually, it's probably more about me than it is about any of them, and certainly more about me than any other story I've written to date.

*"Now whether it was two men that fought in a dark
forest on that fateful night, or whether it was a
man-bull and a were-bear, it is hard to say and harder
still to know."*

Mad Gilly & the Were-Bear

PROLOGUE

*P*rofessor Josiah Loewenstein used the
last of his N.E.H. grant money to have
his Volkswagen towed up the mountain
to the Rockton garage. Even if the engine hadn't
burst into flames, the car would've been of
little use to him now anyway. Not even a fully
loaded SUV could get him up and over Mt. Gil,
the rocky butte towering over the quaint little
Colorado town of Rockton, nestled in the bosom
of the Rocky Mountains. But Mt. Gil was where
Loewenstein was heading.

The next morning he set out, carrying a

canteen, military rations, a sleeping bag, an inflatable raft, a camping knife, and a small digital audio recorder. He also had a snub-nose .38, sent to him by a disreputable old friend. Just in case.

After a two-day hike up and around the mountain, and then a difficult row across the lake beyond it, he found the old man. Upon Loewenstein's arrival, the old man, known only as "Uncle Tim" to the Rockton locals, though no one in town knew quite why, was rocking away on his front porch. He was a desiccated, skeletal figure—to a man what a raisin was to a grape—but he was spry and alert, and happy to receive a visitor. And when Loewenstein explained the purpose of his visit, Uncle Tim could barely contain himself. It had been a long time since he had told anyone the story of Gilmore Gammesson and the founding of Rockton.

Loewenstein accepted a cup of tea from the old man's wife. She was younger, surely, than her husband, but still ancient by any measure.

Loewenstein put the audio recorder on the bench, turned it on, and the old man began...

INTRODUCTION

This here is the story of one Gilmore Gammesson, known as Mad Gilly Games...gambler, drunkard, killer and king, without peer in his time, who reckoned he could live forever. Now you might have already heard this yarn of the most famous son of Rockton, Colorado, but you likely didn't hear it the way I tell it.

Sure, it's got yer gunfights and injun raids, miners and mountain men, a corrupt sheriff and a greedy tycoon, a pretty young thing and an old whore with a heart of gold, and, a course, a handsome, young gun-slinging hero. And it's got t'other parts, too, but if you squint real hard, you can skip right past the demons, dragons and wizards—even the were-bear—if'n you've a mind to. You won't hardly notice them a`tall, most likely. But those parts of the story need a telling, too, even though they oft get left out by the pale, chinless ninnies hereabouts what ain't got the stomach for such notions.

Now don't git me wrong. It's not like I put much stock in such foolishness...after all, who could believe such things? I just think you should hear the whole kit and caboodle and then you can make up your own mind about it, one way or t'other. Besides, even if you don't entertain such notions, you just might find that such notions may entertain you.

So, this is the story, complete and unabridged, as best as I can remember it, and nearly true...or near enough.

THE STORY BEGINS

Some folks like a story to start with blood, so let's begin on the day Gilmore Gammesson rode back into the town of Rockton, what was then called Rook, after a decade spent down in Texas making quite a disreputable name for hisself.

Gammesson had become known as Mad Gilly Games, and since that was what they called him, then that was who he was. Mad Gilly rode back into the town of Rook on a day like any other, astride the legendary horse what Gilly called "Horse". Though Gilly was older now, and dressed in the style of the Texicans of the time, it was not hard for the townsfolk to recognize the return of their golden child. "Gilly's back! Gilly's back!" was the loud whisper that traveled up and down the streets like a wild fire. The blaze burned a trail to the door of the sheriff's office, and so Sheriff Jack "Bull" Evans stepped out into the middle of Main Street to see what set the flame.

Bull Evans was a nasty feller, a former Pinkerton, monstrously tall, bald as an eagle, and with a scarred visage covered by a well-waxed handlebar `stache. Bull had taken a dislike to Gilly even upon his arrival in Rook. When Gilly growed some, he got hisself into a dustup with Evans that would require the boy's hasty departure from the only home he'd ever known. Because when you blow the top of a sheriff's skull clean off, even a dislikable cuss like that Bull Evans, you best be making tracks afore a posse of Pinkertons makes yer departure from the world their sole and solemn purpose.

And now all these years later, here they were again, face to face, despite the unlikelihood of such a reunion. Gilly rode up to face Bull.

"Mad Gilly, get down off that horse. You're under arrest," said the sheriff.

"For what? Killin' ya? Ya ain't even dead!" snarled Gilly, angry and not a little confused by the effrontery of Evans' continulating existence.

"Not for your lack of trying, boy."

"In case ya hadn't noticed, Sheriff, I ain't a boy no more."

Gilly was about to shoot off the top of Evans' head again, when he noticed a great many rifles pointing toward him from a wide range of positions around the street. It appeared that Bull had accumulated some deputies over the years.

"Step down now, Mr. Gammesson," said the sheriff, with a hint of the sneer you knew he carried in his heart for every living thing. Truth be told, Evans did have a fair grudge agin' Gilly, seeing as how the boy had once shot Bull right between his light blue eyes.

Gilly dismounted, slow and easy. Evans went to pull the Colt out of Gilly's holster, but even as he reached over, Horse reared up fast and came down quick with his sharp hooves on the top of Bull's skull, crushing his bald head into the dirt, even as the rest of Bull's body took another moment or so to foller thereafter.

As guns started blazing from everywhere, Gilly reached up to the horn on his saddle, put one foot in the stirrup, and held tight to Horse's flank as Horse bolted down a side alley off the main street. Once they were out of range, Gilly mounted up, circled back and waited in shadows, as the deputies formed a posse to follow him. As soon as they had gathered themselves together in the street, Gilly and Horse were in among `em, with his Colt flashing, and Horse's hooves slashing the air, the both of `em moving and spinning and shooting like a cobra riding a dragon, spitting lead in all directions at once. Soon enough, all those fellers were down, and Gilly was shrieking a blood-curdling whoop. Some said they even saw Horse snort flames that day, but take that how you will.

Gilly got down offa Horse and stood in the middle of the town, ankle deep in guts and glory. "I declare this town free of Bull Evans, and his master, Newton Starr!" he called out. "You folks is now under mah protection!"

Aww, wait a minute now. I think I done left out some things. Getting old has a way of changing the telling of the tale, I s'pose. So let's just take a breath, and step back a might.

Before the story began

I heard tell that Gilmore Gammesson was born the son of a half-breed whore and the Third Cavalry. It was the year of our lord 1850, or thereabouts, when Gilly shot out of his mama's worn cunny as she squatted in the woods near Fort Collins, Colorado. The child emerged with a full head of golden curls, and eyes so black they made the night sky burn dark with envy, and skin so bronze the boy gave off a golden glow when the morning sun hit him just right.

His mama died out there in the woods on that sad eve, but Gilly was rescued by a she-wolf what dragged the child back to her den and suckled him for many a night. That unlikely situation was eventually come upon by a wild feller, one Timothy Dugan by name and a trapper by inclination. Trapper Dugan kilt that wolf, thinking he was saving the child from harm. He stripped the wolf's fur, then cooked and ate her.

The next day, he wrapped baby Gilly in a cavalry blanket he found in the wolf's den, with the name "G. Gammes" scrawled along its ragged fringe. He took the child with him as he continued his journey south along the front ridge of the Rockies. But Trapper Dugan was a solitary sort that preferred to keep his own company. And, though the child was not a whiner, Dugan had his fill of the boy's civilizing effect by the time they came upon a mining camp by the name of Rook, somewhere southwest of Boulder and northeast of Denver. Dugan abandoned little Gilly to the tender maternality of the local whores and hiked hisself up into the icy mountains to the west.

You'll hear more about Trapper Dugan later. As to the next chapter in young Gilly's life, it, too, must be forestalled because I need to tell you this story afore I tell you that story.

THIS STORY...

The town of Rook squatted like a toad in the foothills of the Rockies, agin' the front range of the Colorado Piedmont. Backed up against the mountains to the west, with Pike's Peak looming large in the southern sky, Rook sat in a valley surrounded by the deep forest of Humble's Wood to the south and the Platte River to the north. The town could only be safely approached from the east, by a single trail across the high plains of Eastern Colorado, what used to be Nebraska.

Of course *safe* was a relative term in that time and place. To cross the high plains, you had to cross injun territory. Some folks made it, and some came up just a hair short, so to speak. The traveling got a might easier though after some tribes signed a treaty down at Fort Laramie, whereupon the injuns mostly ignored the settlers and prospectors criss-crossing their hunting grounds, as long as they didn't make themselves too unsightly. Which, upon further consideration, was a hard thing for white folks to do... times being so much different then, a'course.

Before the prospectors started showing up, Rook was home to the Humbaba. They called their home "Uruk," and I can't rightly say for sure what the name means, since I'm only a tad familiar with the Humbabian tongue. But I wouldn't be a bit surprised if it meant "git the hell outta here, you white-skinned devils." Or words to that effect.

Treaty or no, the Hums made it mighty unwholesome for those prospectors and settlers what scurried about on their land. Until one day the Hums found themselves dispossessed of their village by Pinkerton guns hired by a craggy feller that went by the name of Starr...Andrew Newton Starr.

Ole Newt Starr was a wealthy Scotsman what had made hisself a fortune in the new world as sole proprietor of the Starr Mining Company. He'd first brought his strange ways and handsome daughter, Isabelle, to Colorado during the gold rush of `59, and his ambitions left no room for those what had come before him. But his ambition was surely the only big thing about him. You see, Ole Newt suffered from a distinct smallness, of both body and soul.

The Humbaba, on t'other hand, were a brave band, mighty in spirit, and fierce warriors, too. Still, there ain't been a bow or spear ever devised by man that could stand up to a Gatling Gun. And so the massacre of Rook came to be known as the *Battle of Humble's Wood* in the history books. The Hums what survived fled south through the forest, settling on the other side of them woods, disappearing like ghosts into the mountains.

So then, with peace having broke out like a rash, the town belonged to Starr...lock, stock and many a smoking barrel. And in the years that follered, Uruk became a populous, sprawling and rowdy town, mispronounced by visitors and locals alike as "Rook." And since that was what they called it, then that was what it was.

Starr set hisself up on a ranch north of town, on the shore of Lake Thannat, accompanied by his beautiful daughter, Isabelle. Izzie Starr was a piece of work, by all accounts. A tall, pale-skinned, white-haired, red-eyed, finely featured albino, she walked like her feet was too good to touch the ground, and carried herself like a fancy figurine what was spun from sugar. But Izzie was a carnivorous bitch in heat...more mantis than maiden, some said. And the Chinese in town, they called her "the white dragon." Despite it all, Ole Newt loved his daughter...she was the only thing either of them ever loved, most likely.

But Newt and Izzie surely made an unlikely pair. When he walked down Main Street with her following close behind—him dwarfish, wrinkled and ruddy, and her tall, pale and slender—they appeared to form a chalk-white exclamation point with a dark, gnarled dot at its base. Of course, one commented on their resemblance to such a freakishly comical punctuation mark at risk of great personal consequence.

To keep the peace in his domain, Ole Newt made Bull Evans the sheriff of Rook. There were those who claimed that Bull was a demon of some sort, and that Starr was a wizard what had conjured him up from the bowels of Hell. But folks say all kinds of things.

Whether wizard, demon or just a mean little bastard, Ole Newt possessed a preternatural ability to smell out gold and silver ore and, having sniffed it out in the Colorado Piedmont, he made another fortune and turned Rook into a boomtown. The townsfolk either worked in Starr's silver mines or on his timber claims, or they partook in the town's other degrading enterprises, feeding off those what ate, drank, whored and gambled as they passed through on their way to someplace better. The lives of the folk residing in Rook were nasty, brutish and short...and that was the good news.

And Bull Evans, he put the fear of Starr into every soul within his angry grasp. Or nearly every soul, anyways.

<h3 style="text-align:center">...THAT STORY</h3>

So Trapper Dugan left baby Gilly at a whorehouse in Rook, and the infant was taken in by the house madam, a faded beauty by the name of Ninsun, called "Sunny" by friends and clientele. A half-breed herself, she was feeling a might tender after recently losing her own young`un to the pox, so she adopted the strange, golden child. Sunny was known to cast a spell or two in her time, but that boy...well, he surely cast a spell on her. His love just lit her up from the tips of her stubby, reddish-brown toes to the frizzy ends of her wild black mane.

Sunny once had a regular customer by the name of Gilmore whom she recalled with a particular fondness, and, since the infant's blanket was emblazoned with that *G. Gammes*, she named the child Gilmore, Gammes' son. And that boy, Gilly Gammesson, he grew hisself up pretty quick amidst the tumult of Rook.

At the age of eight, Gilly was standing in the middle of the road, chucking cow pies up into the wind, when a funeral procession came upon him. The mortician's man came and shooed the boy out of the way, so the mourners could proceed. Irritated at the interruption, Gilly stood aside and, when the hearse came by, noted "I ain't never gonna be shut in no box forever."

Sid Uhry, the saloon keeper, was standing nearby and said, "You don't plan to be buried, young master Gammesson?"

"No, suh...in fact, I don't plan to die a'tall!"

Sid just laughed. "You are a mad one, young Gilly!" And "Mad Gilly" the town took to calling him that day. And since that was what they called him, then that was who he was.

By age fifteen, Mad Gilly already knowed how to hold his liquor, deal from the bottom, fight dirty and shoot the eyes out of a buffalo nickel. Handsome and a charmer, he was liked by folks, but not WELL liked, if'n you take my meaning. Point of fact, he was more feared than fancied. After all, his mama was a witchy half-breed whore and he was as strong-headed as a mule on loco weed, and twice as dangerous, without the good sense to be afeard of fearful things.

That's when Gilly had his first showdown with Bull Evans, necessitating the boy's leave-taking of Rook. Bull had tried to jail young Gilly for public drunkenness, conducting the arrest with his usual ill temper, but Gilly expressed his objection to Bull's demeanor by pulling his Colt and shooting Bull in the head.

Afore Gilly lit out of town, Sunny gave him a special stone necklace that she claimed had Humbabian powers. He guffawed, but put it on nonetheless. She told him to go to Humble's Wood and find Trapper Dugan. He was the kind of a feller who could be helpful at a time like this. Gilly, not having anywhere else to go and, whatever else he was, still only a scared boy, took Sunny's advice and disappeared into the woods afore Starr's other gunmen could find him. Little did Gilly know what he would find waiting for him out in those woods.

The Coming of Inky Dugan

By the time Gilly came strolling through Humble's Wood on that troubled day, Trapper Dugan had already moved on from the environs of Rook and was nowhere to be found. But he did leave something behind...a son, left in the care of a Humbabian squaw. Now whether she was the child's birth mother or only his wet nurse no one knows for sure, but she was all the mama that boy would ever know. Afore departing, Trapper Dugan had dubbed him "Inky," for the jet black hair that covered most of the child's body and the deep set eyes that sat in his head like bottomless blue-black pools of tar.

And that boy, Inky Dugan, he was raised a Hum. At the ripe ole age of twelve, he was left in the woods by his mama to fend for hisself, as was required by the Humbabian warrior's rite of ascension. She let his hand drop and Inky walked into those woods without a backward glance, and he never returned to the tribe thereafter. Whether that filled the squaw's heart with pain or relief is unknowable, but I'd be acknowledging the corn of it to guess it was both.

So now here was Gilly, on the run, spotting a figure hightailing it through the woods. At first he thought it was a grizz, but then he realized that it was a man what gamboled amongst the thickets, and so he hailed him. "Oyo, Mr. Dugan!" shouted Gilly, thinking the feller to be Trapper Dugan.

Inky froze in his tracks, shocked to hear a human voice calling his name, especially one spouting English...a tongue that generally predicated all sorts of shecoonery. But it was a tongue Inky knowed well enough, as it was taught him by a preacher what had lived briefly among the Hums, before they ate his holy heart. Inky cast his keen eye toward the sound and saw Gilly, standing in and amongst the chaparral.

Inky recognized the boy as not much older than himself, with both of them still between the grass and the hay. Inky quickly took note of Gilly's countenance: Hum-crafted breeches and a tunic, with a strange stone amulet around the neck, and, most tellingly, a low-slung holster strapped to his leg, sporting a smoke pole of potentially devastating effect.

"Trapper Timothy Dugan?" Gilly queried uneasily, confused by Inky's youth.

"Your voice carries well enough without all that wind behind it," sighed Inky, as Gilly walked toward him.

"Oh, mah apologies. I jes' been searchin' for Trapper Dugan. But you ain't him, are ya?" said Gilly, with disappointment.

Inky's eyes got small and his brow furrowed. "And you think searching for him gives you the right to find him, *umgatchni*?"

"Who ya callin' a, a...an Umga-whatzis, ya hairy barbarian?" spat Gilly, with indignation.

Inky kept a hard stare for as long as he could before breaking into a smile. Gilly smiled back. Inky spoke again.

"Well, I am the only Dugan that you are likely to find in these woods. But if you were looking for my father, you must have something important on your mind. So come along. It is time for the evening victuals. We will break some bread, and then you may have your say, before going on your way come morning."

Gilly followed Inky back to his winter cabin, a shabby pile of timber amidst the brambles, near a fresh-water stream. Dugan built a fire and started in on searing a pair of rabbits what he had trapped and skinned earlier in the day.

After dinner, Inky finally spoke. "Well?"

So Gilly told Inky the story of his life to date, such as he knowed it, and such as I've related. Inky responded in kind.

"Is Trapper Dugan really yer pa?" asked Gilly.

"So I was told by the squaw that raised me."

"I always thought of him as mah pa, too. I don't remember him none, but Sunny told me stories 'bout him, and I've seen him in mah dreams many a time."

Inky grunted in response. He then sat silent for a while. "Let me see that necklace of yours," he finally said. Gilly passed it over. Inky studied it closely, then handed it back. "Humbabian talisman. Useful piece of decoration. Do not take it off while you are in these woods. Especially tomorrow night...the moon will be full tomorrow night." Gilly was confused, but pretended to understand.

Inky went on. "You will be followed soon enough by ruffians, so I suggest you get moving in the morning."

"But I got nowhere ta go."

"In that case, one place should be as good as another. You just cannot remain here. I do not want any trouble with the townsfolk. And besides, there are...creatures in these woods... things that I might not be able to protect you from."

Gilly continued to eat in silence. "What if'n I go up into the mountains?"

"It is coming up on winter. You would not last a fortnight up there. I always come down here this time of year, until spring. No, you will want to head south."

"How far?"

"Until you arrive somewhere where you know no one and no one knows you."

"Then what?"

"Then you live your life, my brother."

Their conversation was suddenly interrupted when they were sprung upon out of the night by a cougar of bad temper and even worse judgment. The big cat leapt upon Inky's back from a high perch, and tried to attach itself with its incisors into Inky's massive shoulders. But before it could, Gilly had pulled his Colt and blasted that puss into eternity.

"You are pretty good with that pistol," noted Inky, not put out overmuch by his brush with death.

"Yup. Gun play and poker are two of mah three great gifts!" he chuckled.

"Well then, with those particular talents, I have a sudden notion as to where you might go."

"Where might that be?"

"Head for Texas, Gilly."

The next day, Inky led Gilly to a clearing, and there he bellowed a terrifying howl up into the morning sky. Soon enough, a wild horse came galloping into the break and stopped in front of Inky, nuzzling his shoulder. The creature was as big and black as a night sky in Montana. "This here is my friend...I call him Horse, for only he knows his own true name. Horse, this is Gilmore Gammesson. He and I are brothers. He needs to be on his way, and you are the only one that can help him get as far and as quick as he needs to go. So take care of him, and yourself."

Inky gave Gilly a bear's tooth for good luck, pointed him south, and wished him well. And so Gilly and Horse headed off, but Gilly somehow knew he would see Inky Dugan again one day.

THE LEGEND OF MAD GILLY GAMES

Gilly and Horse arrived in Texas and cut a swath through the killers, con men, cripples, confederates, cattlemen, card sharps and courtesans that were the primary occupants of that territory in those early decades after the War Between the States. Gilly tried his hand at wrangling and rustling, and was equally adept at both. But he didn't like being part of a herd, so mostly he earned his keep by playing cards. His steely nerves, quick mind and unnatural luck, backed up by the lightning thunder of his Colt revolver, made him a legend in those parts. "Mad Gilly Games," he came to be called. And since that was what they called him, then that was who he was.

As he growed hisself into a man, Gilly exercised the third of his three great gifts with uncommon regularity, pirooting many a rancher's daughter, shopkeeper's wife and saloon gal along the trail. He had a way of treating the ladies like whores and the whores like ladies, which was a tendency oft appreciated by both. But he and Horse never settled down too long in any one place. And afore too long, every new town they'd get to, Gilly would find that his reputation had preceded him, sometimes necessitating gunplay that would require his ongoing perambulations.

In this way, years crawlt by until a decade had snuck passed. And after all that time, Mad Gilly Games had kilt enough lads, bedded enough lovelies, and laid down enough winning hands to last him a lifetime or two. A hankering for something else was growing inside him and stabbing at his innards, as if he'd swallered a set of red hot silver spurs. Gilly's skin still glowed bronze, but it had lost its luster. His quick smile had slowed. Too many mornings, it was like he carried a brick in his hat. And so, on one random Texas morning, he and Horse started riding north.

Mad Gilly was going home.

INTERLUDE

Uncle Tim called for his jug. His wife grumbled under her breath, but fetched it nonetheless. He took a long slow swig and then passed it over to Loewenstein. The professor accepted it politely and took a small taste, as a fraternal gesture. The liquor was unfamiliar but quick to burn its way down his gullet. The pain, however, was quickly replaced with a warm sense of well-being that began to grow in the pit of his stomach...a not unpleasant sensation, in fact.

"Not bad, eh?" snickered the old man. "It's Mountain's Blood...an old family recipe. Keeps you young!" The old woman called out from the house, "There ain't enough blood in all the Rockies to keep you young, ya old mountain goat!"

The two men laughed. "Where was I?" the old man queried. "Mad Gilly was going home!" yelled the old woman, from inside. "Oh, yes..." continued the old man.

A Falling Starr

Gilly got down offa Horse and stood in the middle of Rook, ankle deep in guts and glory. "I declare this town free of Bull Evans, and his master, Newton Starr!" he called out. "You folks is now under mah protec—"

Oh, wait. I already done told you that part. So, on we go from there...

There was much rejoicing in Rook on that fine day, which had just seen the sun set a second time on the life of Sheriff Jack Bull Evans. Madame Sunny, so glad to see Gilly alive after all those years in Texas, crushed him agin' her massive bosom. Sid Uhry declared it a holiday, with drinks on the house, and the stagecoach driver, Miss Sharon, pulled Evans' tin star off his bloody corpse and pinned it on Gilly's vest.

Gilly and Horse were a parade all by their own selves, but one that was soon follered by nearly the entire town, right up to the mouth of Newt Starr's main silver mine, the #7. The good folks of Rook had themselves a picnic of an impromptu nature, right there and then. In doing so, they might as well have dropped their drawers and waved their privates at Ole Newt ... which, in fact, some fellers did that night for good measure, after a hog-killing time was had by all.

Now, Andrew Newton Starr was a great many things, but being the sort of feller at whom you waived your johnson was certainly not among `em. And though most of his men were now most grotesquely deceased, thanks to Gilly and Horse, he was not a man without bountiful resources.

He summoned his few remaining ranch hands to collect up the body of Bull Evans. He would have need of it at some point, he knew. In the meantime, he sent a telegram to Kansas City, asking his agent there to start hiring some more guns so he could retake the town. And he would summon his daughter, Isabelle, too. At present, she was visiting the family's holdings back in Scotland, but she could prove useful at a time like this.

The Were-Bear Strikes

Gilly may have been mad, but he was in no way stupid. He knew that it was one thing to take a town, and quite another to hold it. And so he enlisted the townsfolk in the efforts to fortify Rook from Newt Starr's inevitable retaliation. His plan: to build a great wall on the town's eastern border, allowing the unfordable waters to the north, unscaleable mountains to the west, and the dangerous beasts and injuns of Humble's Wood to the south, to defend Rook's other three sides. Atop the fence would be a tower with a complete view of the town, to be manned by men with Gatling Guns, to guard the gate.

After all, it's been said that good fences make good neighbors, and Gilly was determined to make Newt Starr the bestest dern neighbor the town of Rook would ever have.

The wall would be a great undertaking, requiring every able bodied man in town to help to cut massive timbers in Humble's Wood, haul them to the eastern line, then saw, shape and assemble them into a fence and tower, with a mighty gate sufficient to hold off a frontal assault. And the townsfolk were willing to do it, too...for a time.

But with his newfound authority, Gilly had a bit of trouble keeping hisself on the straight and narrow, tending to abuse his privileges at the expense of those entrusted to his protection. So, while fellers were off hacking down trees, he was bedding down their womenfolk with alarming frequency. Such was his charm that he would never take by force what was freely given; still, 'twas an insult not kindly thought of and made many in the town uneasy.

He earned further ill will by his nightly drunken rides through the streets of Rook, with Gilly shooting out windows and Horse tearing up vegetable gardens and knocking down porches. Those that objected found themselves on their backs, staring up at the stars through blackened eyes, just past a broken nose.

Gilly also had a nasty habit of winning poker pots with freakish regularity, much to the consternation of the town's burghers, who were required to sit in with him for at least a few hands each night, over at Sid Uhry's Saloon.

To stand up to Mad Gilly was to get the wrong pig by the tail and, in the days and weeks that follered, townsfolk were starting to miss Bull Evans.

Then, one day a timber crew returned from Humble's Wood with a frightening tale. They had been set upon by the biggest grizzly ever seen in them parts. It attacked them and ate off poor Samuel Butt's arm, and clawed a few others in the crew, afore they could make it back to town. The creature had even left a tooth in the leg of young Kwai Chang. When Gilly examined the tooth, he realized he had worn its identical twin round his neck, nestled alongside his talisman, for the past ten years. So, it would be up to Gilly now to go into the woods and hunt that bear, whose name he suspected he already knowed.

Horse took Gilly back to the clearing in Humble's Wood where once Gilly had sat and eaten rabbits with Inky Dugan. There they waited. It did not take long. Inky had growed even bigger since last they met, standing nearly twenty hands high now, as thick around the chest as a Longhorn steer measures from tip to tip, and able to crush a grizzly in a bear hug, if'n he were of a mind to do such a thing. In fact, with his habit of wearing pelts and maintaining his overlong black tresses in an unkempt manner, Inky suggested a big ole grizz hisself, to those few what crossed his path and lived to tell the tale.

"Howdy, Inky."

"Welcome back, Gilly."

"I think ya done ate one o` my timber crew."

"Possibly. All white men taste alike to me."

"Well, I need ya to stop."

"With Hums being so scarce these days, and your townsfolk being so suddenly plentiful in my woods, I take what I can get," sighed Inky.

"So how come yer not eatin' me right now, then?" asked Gilly, his eyes narrowing.

Inky smiled and pointed at the stone talisman around Gilly's neck. Gilly drew his Colt and clicked back the hammer.

"Brother, I don't wanna shoot ya none, but these people are under mah protection."

Inky laughed, throwing his head back in a wild howl that sent chills up Gilly's spine. "You think you can harm me with lead? Then take your best shot, little man." He roared with defiance and charged. Gilly pulled the trigger on his black-eyed Susan, speeding a bullet toward Inky. It struck its mark, but without effect. Inky stopped and howled with laughter again.

"No bullets forged by man can pierce my hide," said the were-bear, "and I have never been bested in battle."

"Well, we'll jes' have to settle this the old fashioned way, then, and see where the chips fall," said Gilly, as he unstrapped his leather and came toward Inky with fisticuffs raised.

And so the two men fought a fight that no one witnessed, 'cept the sky and the stars and the trees and the hills, and yet here I am here to tell you that it was a battle for the ages, raging through the night and into the following dawn. Gilly, though much smaller than Inky, was inhumanly quick, surprisingly strong and tougher than jerky, and gave a good account of hisself. When the sun broke through the morning mist, the rays danced upon Gilly's bronze skin and golden curls, dappling him like an Appaloosa and giving off an otherworldly glow that momentarily blinded the exhausted Inky Dugan. Gilly summoned his remaining strength and landed one last mighty blow that lifted the massive bear-man off his feet and into darkness.

When Inky awoke, he found his wounds being tended to by Gilly, who raised a drink to Inky's lips. "I am yours, brother...forever," Inky said, before taking a light sip.

"Hush now. Rest up. I'm takin' ya back into town with me. I need ya by mah side."

"Wherever you lead, I will follow, until darkness takes us both."

"Yeah, well, good luck to the darkness that comes a lookin' for us, eh?" laughed Gilly.

The Plot Unfolds

Mad Gilly had stolen Newton Starr's crown. It would be weeks afore Ole Newt would have the strength of numbers to reclaim it, and months 'til the summer solstice, when he could conjure the return of Bull Evans to lead his men in such an endeavor. In the meantime, Izzie Starr had a plan. She would seduce this new king and Gilly would then be hers, and he would be made to serve her father's will. But Ole Newt didn't want to take the chance of leaving Gilly alive, where he could still turn on Starr one day, despite his daughter's undeniable charms.

"Acch, Izzie," Newt sputtered in his unmistakable brogue, "we need a more permanent solution to our problem. There is one fellow who might be able to terminate Mr. Gammesson for us...a giant, half-breed mountain man known as Inky Dugan. He used to live down in Humble's Wood, but now he lives in town, as Gammesson's deputy. Go to him; work your magick upon him, capture his heart. Then, cast your spell on Mr. Gammesson, too. When jealousy brings the two of them into conflict, it will not be the first time such a thing had happened in the history of men. If Dugan kills Gammesson, our problem will be solved. And if Gammesson kills Dugan, it will leave him alone and broken, and still our problem will be solved."

"Why would Gilly be so put out by the killing of some half-breed?" asked Izzie. "I've heard that he has killed dozens of men, and at least twice as many redskins."

"Dugan is not just anybody. He and Gammesson are brothers of a sort."

"Of what sort would that be, Da?"

"It's a long story. Just do it, me dear. I'm sure the doings will provide you with sufficient entertainment to justify your efforts."

Izzie Starr considered her father's request, as she bathed in the chilly waters of Lake Thannat, glistening like a highland snowbird on its still surface. She was most at home here in the water, as in the lochs of her youth. It was where she was most herself. *Yes,* she thought. *Yes, let us do entertain the gentlemen.* She laughed, and her laughter made birds take wing, and insects chitter, and forest creatures seek higher purchase.

BROTHERS OF ROOK

At first, the townsfolk were terrified of their new resident, a monstrous creature in human form. But when they saw the effect that Inky had on Gilly, they privately rejoiced. Gilly and Inky drank together, laughed together, and worked together overseeing the security of the town. Despite his bestial appearance, Inky had a surprisingly civilizing effect on Gilly, who tended now toward rational discourse rather than impetuous outbursts.

When the moon waxed full, the two brothers retreated to Humble's Wood, and Inky ran free to hunt and feed, clothed only in the coat of black fur that would thicken and cover him at such times, while Gilly kept hold of his talisman and sat round the fire, waiting for the days and nights to pass until the moon waned again and Inky would return to hisself... although Inky reckoned he was more hisself at the apex of the moon than at any other moment of his life.

And so it went in the town of Rook. As work continued on the fortifications, and the menfolk commenced training under the leadership of their golden sheriff and his hirsute deputy, the community came together in a time of grace that it had not known since Rook was Uruk, a home only to horses and Hums. And Gilly and Inky found in each other kinship they had never knowed.

Until one midday, when into their midst rode Isabelle Starr on a white mare, upon which she sat side saddle in the English manner, carrying a parasol for shade. When she walked into Uhry's Saloon, Inky was knocked back like a cocked hat. For, as powerful a creature as he was, he was the only one of his kind as far as he knew, and he had not known any woman's touch since his mother had slipped loose of his hand that fateful day in the woods. He had certainly never seen a woman of Isabelle's comely nature. So, he was unprepared for the flood of emotion that overwhelmed him in that moment.

When the lady strode in, Inky was seated alone at a table, playing solitaire and drinking rotgut. Isabelle sat down beside him. "You are Gilly's friend, are you not?" Inky was unable to speak.

She extended her hand. "I am Isabelle Starr; delighted to make your acquaintance." Inky took her delicately gloved hand in his massive paw and shook it gently.

"My, you are quite a specimen, Mr. ...Mr. ...?"

"Dugan, ma'am. Inky Dugan."

"Oh, how delightful! Inky! Yes, it suits you. And where is your friend... Mr. Gammesson?"

Inky pointed toward the rooms upstairs, where Gilly was taking one of Sunny's new girls out for a hard ride.

"Oh, yes, I see," said Isabelle, as she poured them both a drink from the bottle on the table. She raised her glass. "*Tir nam Beann, 's nan Gleann, 's nan Gaisgeach!*" she toasted, then downed the shot without hesitation. "Cheers," said Inky, and followed suit. And so it went.

Soon they were laughing and sharing intimacies, with Izzie reaching over and playfully twirling Inky's black chest hairs in her long white fingers. Inky was more intoxicated by her than the whiskey. Soon enough, they, too, were in a room upstairs, thrashing about like rutting beasts in heat.

When Inky fell asleep, drained and exhausted, Izzie dressed and slipped out. Downstairs she found Gilly, chatting with Sid Uhry at the bar. Their eyes locked. Gilly had known Isabelle since his childhood days in Rook. She smiled, but her eyes betrayed a reptilian quality that raised the little hairs on the back of his neck.

"Well, well...Mad Gilly. Welcome home," Izzie said.

"Yeah, yer daddy's boys sure gave me a real `welcome home', alright. So what're ya doin' in mah town, Miss Starr?"

"Why Gilly, you can't possibly think I give a hoot about daddy's minions. Or about who controls this spittoon of a town."

"No? Then what are ya here fer?"

"I'm here for YOU, Gilly." She kissed him and he let hisself get kissed. He could smell her, and it was a smell that filled his senses like a bouquet of poppies. He could feel his desire overwhelming his distrust. And soon enough the two were upstairs again, rolling around in the room next door to the one where Inky still slept.

Now, as regarding the third of Gilly's three great gifts, folks said that Gilly was even better at pokin' than poker, and when he got Izzie to hit high C, it was she what got trapped in her own snare. Suddenly she was not only wanton, but wantin', and her daddy's intrigues went flying out the window. She was blinded by golden curls, and caressed by bronze skin, and falling into black eyes that went on and on forever.

But the next thing she knowed, a massive paw had grabbed her by her white tresses and was dragging her, buck nekkid, out of the bed, across the room, down the stairs, out the saloon and into the street. She screamed and tried to pull free, but Inky Dugan barely noticed her efforts.

Dugan hauled her up to her horse and tossed her over the saddle onto her belly, as she continued to writhe like a sackful of diamondbacks. He tied her hands and feet together under the horse, as she let fly with a tirade of foul language that, while unbefitting a lady of her stature, was surely appropriate to her situation. Inky whispered to the horse, "take her home," then slapped her flank...the horse's flank, that is. And off went the snowy mare, cantering up Main Street, back to the Starr ranch. Izzie's screams and vituperations grew fainter, as did the glare of the sun off the milky white buttocks of both horse and passenger, as they disappeared into the distant hills.

Inky walked back into Uhry's saloon and sat down at the table where Gilly sat, waiting. Gilly filled their glasses. Inky pushed the cards over to Gilly. "Deal," he said.

Charge of the Forty Guns

"Destroy them, Da...destroy them now!" shrieked Isabelle.

Old Newt was angry. His town had been taken, his men killed, his mines shut down, and now his daughter publicly humiliated. He was a man of power, of means, who was used to getting his way, and he had been utterly thwarted by that son of a whore and his friend, the half-breed bear-man. So when I speak to you of his anger, you can't even imagine the depths and the height of it. But compared to the rage of Izzie Starr, his was but a dim spark next to a conflagration.

"Be reasonable, me dear. I must wait until the solstice to perform the ritual, and—"

"I don't care about your silly rituals! You have hired enough new men. Use them!"

"We need Bull Evans to lead them. Without him, they are just forty men with guns."

"But Gilly and Inky are just two men!"

"Two, yes...but men? No, I don't think so...not entirely."

"Da, I did as you asked and this was the result. Now do this for me, or so help me..."

"Yes dear, I—"

"...I will not be responsible for the consequences!"

"I understand, me dearie. The moon disappears from the night sky only six weeks hence, upon the summer solstice, and I swear to you, on that night the Bull shall rise and our enemies shall fall!"

"Six weeks? SIX WEEKS!? *Hrummph!*" Izzie stormed off, not overjoyed by her father's cool response to her burning need for immediate retribution.

Finally, six weeks slunk by and, in the dark night of the new moon, Ole Newt berobed hisself with the accoutrements of his office: a velveteen cape, a pointed cap, and a bejeweled staff carved from an ancient wood that no longer grew upon the Earth. He spoke sacred words from an ancient text over the decayed and headless corpse of Bull Evans. And even as the old man's sonorous incantations sung out over Lake Thannat, something stirred deep beneath its waters, causing waves to ripple across its bubbling surface.

Evans' corpse started to shake and glow. Gradually, the head of a great bull emerged from the body's neck stump, with deadly horns blossoming like ivory flowers atop the skull, and a snout rising from the bovine face like a feller's manhood at first light. The body's shriveled feet grew into great cloven hooves, as the body's decaying flesh reconstituted itself from the stuff of air, and earth, and water, and flame. Bull Evans stood up from the stone table on which he had been laid, his Bull's head now towering nearly eight feet above the ground.

"Go, oh great bull, and destroy our enemies," spake the velveteen dwarf. "Circle around Rook and take the southern road up through Humble's Wood. You will come out behind their mighty gate and take them by surprise. When the brothers have fallen, open the gate. I shall then send in the forty guns to help you take back the town."

The Bull roared and stampeded off into the night. Ole Newt stood on a chair to hang up his cape and hat and put away his staff and book. He then readied his gunmen to ride on the town. *Where is Izzie?* he wondered, amidst the hubbub. *She would so enjoy this glorious moment!*

The Bull and the Bear

The Great Bull made its way down the road, passing by the southern tip of Lake Thannat. There he saw a shadow emerge from the water. It was the lady, Isabelle, who somehow glistened on that moonless night. She called to him. "Come to me, Bull. I have a gift for you." Bull heeded her command. "Kneel before me." He did. She reached into the water and scooped some mud from the lake bed. She whispered some words over the dark wet earth in her hands, and then rubbed the mud over the horns of the great beast. "Any son of man gored by your horns shall die in slow, writhing agony. Now go!"

The Bull was soon enough strolling through the heart of Humble's Wood. White men wisely avoided that trail, afeared as they were of the Hums and the beasts residing there. But The Bull knew no fear. He knew only the scent of blood, the stench of which rose in his great snout. He uprooted a smallish tree along the way, pulling off its branches and leaves, shaping it with his sharp hooves, fashioning hisself a club. You see, since he was still part man, the Bull felt nekkid without a weapon in his hands. And, so armed, he stumbled loudly through the woods toward the town, making no secret of his coming.

It was Inky that sensed it first. He awoke with a start. He heard the call of drums, though whether they were coming from the woods or from inside his own head, as a reminder of his late night debauching, he was not certain. He looked in on Gilly, who was a snoring like ole Epharim the she-bear. Inky let his brother sleep on. *I'll check on this myself. No need to involve Gilly just yet*, he thought, as he crept out the rooms of Sunny's bawdyhouse, where the two had taken up permanent residence. He follered the drums south, off the main street and towards the woods.

Now whether it was two men that fought in a dark forest on that fateful night, or whether it was a man-bull and a were-bear, it is hard to say and harder still to know. What was clear, though, was the bloody aftermath, which Gilly stumbled upon after following Inky's trail some time later. The headless body of Bull Evans was laying on a rock, with the bull's head spilt out over the forest floor. And, nearby, Inky sat up against a tree, trying to catch his breath.

"Inky, watcha doin' out here, fightin' with that bullheaded son of Hell, all by yer lonesome?"

"I did not wish to disturb you, Gil. But it is alright, I took him."

Gilly looked down and saw the blood oozing from Inky's side. "Yeah, but it looks like he done took ya back! Let's get ya home, to Sunny. She'll fix ya up good."

Gilly got Inky up on Horse, as gentle as he could, and they rode back into town. Inky was laid down on a bed and Sunny tended to him. But after a while, she turned to Gilly and said, "My son, the wound cannot be healed. He is bewitched by a poison that I cannot defeat."

"Ma, there must be somethin' you can do. He cain't die!"

"Yes, he can. And so can you." Now that news struck Mad Gilly Games like a lightning bolt. It had never occurred to him that he could die. He was the golden child. Surely he would live forever, he thought.

"You and Inky are not gods, Gilly. You are men, mostly. And it is the blessing of the great mother that men can die. So be glad, not afeared. For those that do not know death, do not know life. And Inky has lived a life of awe and wonder. As have you, my son."

"But it cain't be over yet, Ma. It just cain't." Gilly sobbed and was shocked by the sound. He hadn't cried over his own mama dying at the moment of his birth, nor upon any occasion since, but here he was now, bawling like a child lost in the dark.

"Gilly, I will tell you again what I told you once before. Go up to the mountains. Find Trapper Dugan. He might be helpful at a time like this. But don't be long about it. Inky doesn't have much time left."

"How long?"

"A day...two, maybe. Now ride!" Hanging on to the thinnest thread of hope, Mad Gilly hopped on Horse and galloped toward the Eastern Gate, carrying Bull's head by his side, as Sunny instructed. The gate was opened for his passing and he rode north and west, into the foothills. So distracted was he, he did not see the forty gunmen waiting on the distant horizon. Upon the gate's opening, the forty guns charged!

MAD GILLY'S QUEST

Not knowing what bloody doings lay behind them, Mad Gilly and Horse burned the wind across the northern foothills, before having to slow their pace as they climbed higher into the jagged, frozen mountains. He would have to find Trapper Dugan afore long or the trip would be for naught. And so, that night, Gilly built a bonfire, setting off a blaze that could be seen from the highest peak in the Rockies. As he suspected, it drew Dugan to him.

"Hey, boy, I heard tell you was looking fer me," said Trapper Dugan.

"Howdja know?"

"I got my ways. Between the Hums drumming, the guns riding, and the wizard spellificating, I just knew you'd find yer way to me, one way or t'other."

"It's Inky. He's in a bad way, Pa, and Sunny said—"

"I ain't YER pa, boy."

"Yeah, I know, but—"

"I'm Inky's pa."

"Well, Inky's my brother, so that makes you SOMETHIN' to me, don't it?"

"Alright...how bout you settle for `uncle', then?"

"If that's what you'll have me call ya, then that's who ya are, I s`pose."

"So what happened to my boy, then?" asked Dugan, and Gilly related the recent doings.

"Mountain's Blood...he needs Mountain's Blood. The injuns say it can cure any ailment, even ones of magical origin, and can even slow down the aging of men."

"Where can I find it at?"

"Well, that's the trick, ain't it, nephew Gilmore?"

"You don't know where it is, do ya?"

"Oh, I do, I do...I just don't know if I should be telling you, is all. You and Inky is my only kin, after all, and it would be a mortal sin to put such a burden on you both."

"I've done enough sinnin' in my life fer all of us, Uncle. So don't you worry `bout that. Now jes' tell me how to find it."

And so Dugan did and, having done so, vanished once again back into the mountains without another word, for either good or ill, him being an unsentimental and dignified sort.

Gilly rode off north, as Dugan instructed, to Lake Thannat. He arrived at daybreak and was shocked to find Ole Newt...dead. Dead and hard as a trail biscuit. Newt, it seems, had petrificated while staring out at the lake from a rocking chair on his porch. Some say he suffered a heart attack when he saw Gilly ride up with the head of the great bull. Others think that Izzie Starr, murderously impatient with her da's failure to defend her honor in a timely manner, done witched the juice right out of him, or some such mumbo jumbo.

At any rate, Gilly shook off his shock at Newt's hardified condition and proceeded down the path from the ranch house to the lake. Dugan had tole him that Mountain's Blood could only be made from a weed that grew in fresh water below a new mountain. He had instructed Gilly to take the Bull's head and throw it into Lake Thannat, to start the process.

Lucky for Gilly that Dugan left unsaid what happened next, or he'd likely never have gone and done as he was tole. You see, when the bull's head hit the water, Isabelle emerged from the depths of the lake, howling. Her burning hate caused the water to boil like a cauldron, and, no longer held in check by her father's magick, she reverted to her true and terrible nature. She arose from the water a great white serpent, big as the hills nearby, with gusts of flame shooting out of her bristling nostrils, which were flared by the presence of her most hated love, one Mad Gilly Games.

Now Gilly had never lacked for nerve, but this was something else again. What could he possibly do agin' such a creature? Nothing else occurred to him, so he drew his pistol and, with five beans in the wheel, let fly. All the bullets struck home but made little impression. It was like barking at a knot. Izzie roared and came forward. Her giant head swooped down, and she swallered Gilly up whole, in a single gulp.

Lesser men might have been discouraged by such a turn of events but, inside the gullet of the serpent, Gilly had one last card to play. He took Sunny's talisman from round his neck and stuck Inky's bear tooth into the notch in its hilt. He then stabbed it, tooth first, with all his might, deep into the tender innards of the beast's gullet, using the butt of his Colt to hammer it home. The dragon Isabelle, violated in this unseemly way, staggered and then vomited Gilly back up onto the shore. She stumbled again, then stood up and, upon doing so...the mighty serpent froze into stone.

Yep, you heard me right. I said stone.

And so, thanks to Humbabian magic, a new peak had been added to the Colorado Piedmont...a great white butte rising up out of the edge of Lake Thannat that would, in later years, come to be called Mt. Gil. And just beneath it, rising up from the mountain's afterbirth, could be found a weed of great and terrible power.

INKY DUGAN GOES HOME

Gilly and Horse rode back to Rook as if death itself was chasing them, but, in point of fact, 'twas the other way round. Death, however, rode a faster, paler horse that day. By the time they arrived, Inky had passed on... as had all of Starr's gunmen, who were strewn about the town in various states of ghastly repose.

You see, the townsfolk had learned well to defend themselves, what with their great wall and the training that Gilly and Inky had provided them. And with no Bull to lead them, Newt's men were just men with guns, going up agin' angry fellers defending their homes and loved ones. It should go without saying that those gunmen got totally exfluncticated. But there, I said it anyway, lest there be some doubt.

Gilly was grief stricken and heartbroken upon witnessing Inky's lifeless body, still lying there in Sunny's bed. But, in that tragic moment, the town took Gilly to its bosom, offering up profound condolences for what he had lost, but deep gratitude, too, for what he led them to find within themselves.

The next morning, Gilly, Sunny, Sid Uhry, Miss Sharon and the other townsfolk follered Inky Dugan's casket deep into Humble's Wood. It was more Inky's home than anywhere on Earth and was the only proper resting place for his mortal remains. Words were spoke over the grave by an itinerant preacher, but they felt hollow. Gilly then dropped into the grave the weeds he had collected at the lake, below the new mountain. He would have no truck with them now.

Then, as if coming out of the trees themselves, there appeared the Hums. Folks were afeared of reprisal, but none was forthcoming. An elder of the tribe came forward and began singing and dancing around the open grave, as some of the Hums banged on drums. After a bit, a tiny roar could be heard from the hole and out climbed a grizzly cub, stumbling on shaky legs. It looked around, sniffed the air, and then scampered off toward the mountains without a backwards look. The sight filled Gilly's heart.

Soon enough, the Hums disappeared back into the woods and the townsfolk drifted back to their homes and back to their lives. Hums were never seen again in these parts, nor any demons, dragons, wizards or were-bears…at least, no sightings that folk would ever admit to.

CONCLUSION

Gilmore Gammesson spent his remaining days in Rook. While he was held in high esteem, he never did take a wife nor did he ever make another friend. When Sunny finally passed away, Gilly buried her near Inky. He would, on pleasant Sunday afternoons, picnic upon their graves. He would, on occasion, hike up into the mountains, too, but he never saw any sign of Trapper Dugan, nor the bear cub that would've growed itself into a dangerous ole grizz by that time.

Some say Gilly died in the flash flood what almost swept Rook off the map some years later. A grave marker was placed next to Inky and Sunny by the town (then called Rockton), signifying as such.

In later years, they even put up a little plaque commemorating his life on the last standing timber of the Eastern Wall, now preserved by the Rockton Chamber of Commerce.

But others say Gilly never did die, because he knew the secret of Mountain's Blood and would stay alive forever, living in Humble's Wood and guarding the secret of the elixir.

Either way, Mad Gilly is still spoken of, his tale still a part of the town and a part of the folks hereabouts. He's called the hero of Rockton, and because that is what they call him, then that is who he is, to this very day.

And so, you see, it's true…Mad Gilly Games lives forever. Not all men die, you know.

Well, that's my story anyway, and I'm sticking to it.

EPILOGUE

"And you, I suppose, are Uncle Tim Dugan, staying alive on Mountain's Blood all these years?" queried Loewenstein, bemusedly.

The old man laughed. The old woman cackled. "It's just a tall tale, perfesser.

Take it for what it's worth."

"I will, Mr. Dugan, I will. I just wonder what it is worth to you, now that you've become part of the tale as well."

"Hmm? Me?"

"Yes, the story will be published in a book. Only an academic press, but still..."

"A book? You don't say!"

The old man considered that. He shared whispers with the old woman, then the couple fell silent for a long time. Finally, the old woman kissed the old man gently on the forehead. He turned and handed the jug to Loewenstein. "I reckon I won't need this anymore, then."

The old man looked up at Loewenstein with a mixture of sadness and relief, turned, and walked slowly into the house. His wife smiled kindly at Loewenstein and followed her husband inside.

Loewenstein walked back down the path, starting the long hike home. The jug was nestled securely in his pack, next to the .38. When he returned to the university, he would have the contents of the jug analyzed. But, upon doing so, he would be utterly unsurprised to learn of the liquid's benign, unremarkable chemistry.

After all, he already knew that was not where the magic lived.

Mad Gilly & the Were-Bear
Author's Note

One of my fondest recollections of childhood was the night my parents let me stay up late on a school night to watch *Cat Ballou*. I've been a fan of westerns (and Jane Fonda) ever since. So when I started working on this collection, I very much wanted to try writing a tale of the Old West, and the "weird western" fantasy sub-genre seemed like my way in. But a weird western about what, exactly?

I had stumbled over the Gilgamesh legend many times in the course of my literary perambulations and, even though it had been adapted often in various genres, I hadn't ever seen it used as the basis of a western, so I chose it as possible source material. *Gilgamesh* is the 'Ur'-text for heroic fantasy literature, but what I love about it is that, at its heart, it's a buddy story...a Butch & Sundance kind of thing. And despite its hero's failed attempt to gain immortality, it is in the very fact that the story survives after thousands of years that Gilgamesh ultimately obtained the immortality he desired. So it's very much a story about the power of a story. I also liked the idea of this Middle Eastern legend forming the core of a Western...that it would be an Eastern Western.

I wanted the story to be true not only to Gilgamesh but to the vernacular of the West, in that time and place. I tried for historical and geographic accuracy where I could, and I wove western slang throughout the telling (along with some stuff I just made up) to give it verisimilitude and its own voice. In doing so, I found myself employing that uniquely American mythic western form, the "Tall Tale", a story type which consciously acknowledges its own preposterous fictionality.

It's also a story that allowed me to use the word *exfluncticated*, which was reason enough to write it.

"Gilly" was published by *Scareship* (December, 2012), and later reprinted by 9*Tales From Elsewhere*, *v.2* (February, 2015). Both these publications were of a slightly shorter version of the story, that didn't contain the "Loewenstein" framing device. For me, however, the story of Mad Gilly is a story about the power of storytelling and the magic inherent in the telling and the listening. I felt the framing device was essential, so here it is.

"Red as flame, with wings edged in yellow, and with azure eyes that bespoke something wonderful behind them, she would soar across the steel-gray sky, drawn always from her nest toward love."

The Firebird:
A Fairy Tale

Loewenstein collected this tale long ago while in a parallel universe (or so he claimed), told to him by a fellow he referred to only as "the man in the high castle." When pressed to explain further, he demurred.

– Editor

T he woman had been picking flowers at the foot of the mountain. The chore took greater effort than it used to in her youth, but flowers made the stress of farm life endurable. Having filled her basket, she started off for home to get supper started for her family.

As she strolled down the mountain path back towards the farm, she heard the wail of a baby coming from the nearby bushes. Alarmed, she ran toward the unsettling sound without a moment's hesitation. Pushing through the brush, she came into a clearing. There she saw a large woven basket sitting in the middle of a large ring of black ashes. In the basket was a crying baby wrapped in a colorful blanket. She knelt down to look more closely. The child was raven-haired and looked up at her with painfully blue eyes. She picked up the infant and soothed him until he was calmed.

As she rocked him, she noticed a letter in the basket. *Supper can wait,* she thought, and, as the baby gurgled in her arms, she sat down on the hard ground and began to read...

I am *J'ol*. Please forgive my shaky hand, as my circumstances are dire and my time is short. If you are reading this, then you have found my child. As I write these words, I cling to the hope that he is still well and that, having found him, you will care for him. Once you know who he is and how he came to you, I feel that you will. I pray that you will. I know that you will.

I am of the *Krye'Dyn*. Our clan lives in a valley on the other side of the mountain. I do not know the nature of your world but magic abides in mine. River sprites keep the fish swimming and the fresh water flowing, goblin gnomes maintain the land and raise food from the earth, elves hunt the wild borders of our domain to keep our larders filled, dwarves mine the mountain for the ore that gives us power, and faeries of the deep wood leave a dew in their wake that we use to maintain our vigor and youth. The Krye'Dyn are the clan of men charged to protect all who live in the valley from those would prey upon us, keeping us safe from the dangers without and within.

I am a seer. I know the ways of the river, the earth, the wood, the wild, and the mountain...the mountain most of all. I can sometimes see through the eyes of men and beasts and so my vision reaches beyond our valley. It is an ancient talent, but not all men have this power. In fact, I am the only one of my people that still has the sight. It has given me a special kinship with the mountain and the animals that reside in our realm. From where does my power come? Who can say? Perhaps the sight is simply a gift of love, bestowed by life itself.

Surely it was love that drew my mate, *La'ar*, to me and to my simple cabin on the side of the mountain, where we live apart from the rest of our folk.

It was love, too, that first drew the Firebird to me. The great bird lived atop the mountain's highest peak, near the black, smoking hole at its summit. Red as flame, with wings edged in yellow, and with azure eyes that bespoke something wonderful behind them, she would soar across the steel-gray sky, drawn always from her nest toward love.

It was through the blue eyes of the Firebird that I first saw the world beyond the mountain... your world. It seemed so close to us, just over the crest, but it was an illusion, a trick of the mind and the light, like a rainbow. Yours is a world that exists an infinite distance from here, and to climb the mountain and step over the ridge is to pass through a doorway into your realm from which no one had ever returned. The Firebird knew this instinctively and, though her flight would often take her near the mountain's ridge, she would never cross the threshold. No one did.

Yes, there were ancient tales of men and beasts that crossed over ages ago, never to return...myths about one-eyed giants, uni-horned equines and great flying lizards that once prowled our valley but have long since vanished from here. But these are just stories that our people tell the wee ones at bedtime. They are not like the Firebird, who flies our sky even as I sit here now.

The Firebird visited me often over the years. Once having seen through her eyes, we were bonded by it as nothing else could. I had seen her wither with age and then return to her nest to die. At the moment of death, she would burst into flames that consumed naught but herself, then she arose from her own ashes, a newly emerged thing of wing and fire, flying out of her nest, ascending into the vault of heaven. Afterwards, she would return to me and perch on my shoulder, nuzzling me for a fairy nut, as if nothing had occurred. And the cycle of the Firebird had repeated itself since before the time of the Krye'Dyn, since the world was young and the mountain first rose out of the primordial sea.

Then the day came when the Firebird flew to me and I could see what she had only just then beheld...the mountain's peak, now a roiling cauldron of burning, smoking, liquid rock. A disaster was in the making; the valley was in peril.

As the seer, it fell to me to advise the council in all things. Sometimes they heeded my words and sometimes they did not. I was held in awe but not trusted, as my sight was unreliable, or so they claimed. I was respected but not liked, as I said things that my people did not always wish to hear. The skill to reason was not highly valued in the valley; where magic lives, rationality is a quaint and unnecessary talent, a vestige of our primitive past.

And while the Krye'Dyn were a good folk and mighty warriors, they only looked at that which was close enough to kill or kiss; their sight of far off things was blurred and dull, and so they paid them no mind. That is why they had me... to see all that they could not, or would not, to be a voice of reason in a realm where magic is reliable and logic is deemed otherwise.

When I told the council of the catastrophe on the horizon, they ignored their mad old wizard and went about their business. After all, there were borders to protect, a river to fish, and fairy dew to brew into deliciously potent *gr'gg*. Tomorrow would have to take care of itself, for the people of the valley were otherwise engaged.

I gave them fair warning. The mining of the dwarves had injured the mountain. If they did not stop pillaging it for ore, the summit would eventually erupt with a fury and a vengeance that would doom the valley and all who resided here. But it was not too late; if the mining stopped now, the mountain could still heal itself. But none would listen. The power derived from the ore was the power of our people and they would not slow its pursuit.

Even later, when a cataclysm became inevitable, I pleaded for the council to plan a retreat from the valley and find a home for us all on the barren plains beyond the gorge to the east. But who would ever choose to abandon the idyllic life of the valley for those hard lands? Surely not the council of the Krye'Dyn. They had unshakeable faith that magic would protect us...after all, it always had.

But I am a creature of both faith and reason, and so I made plans to leave the valley. La'ar and I would travel east and somehow survive on the distant plains. It was a difficult journey, with no guarantee of safety beyond the gorge, but there was no alternative. To remain meant death. Of that, reason left no doubt.

Sadly, our trip was not to be. To our great surprise, La'ar discovered that she was with child. She and I were not young by any measure, and such a thing seemed beyond us at that point, so we were shocked by the news, but delighted, too. Parenthood was something that had been denied us in our life together, but now it was being visited upon us at our eleventh hour. We were going to be a family, so now more than ever an escape was necessary, but we were unlikely to sustain ourselves on an arduous journey to a distant land with La'ar in this condition. We would have to wait and pray that the mountain would give us the time we needed to make our way to safety.

The baby came, as babies often do. La'ar had given me a son and she had named him *K'eL*, after her father, in the tradition of the Krye'Dyn. The infant had jet black hair, with an adorable curl falling down upon his forehead. His eyes were almost inhumanly blue, like his mother's, and brighter even than those of the Firebird.

K'eL was but a few months old when the Firebird returned, drawn back to us by the power of our love for the child. But she did not come to bring us gifts or good wishes, or to beg for nuts. Instead, she came with a vision that was terrifying in its inevitability.

Lava had started to overflow the rim at the peak. An eruption was coming. We had to flee, but there was no time. The valley was too wide and deep, and the imminent explosion of the mountain would be too soon and too great to evade. Earthquakes had already begun and tremors caused the gorge to collapse and so there was no way out of the valley any longer. We would all drown in a bowl of molten rock and burning ash and noxious fumes. The lucky few would die quickly.

I thought La'ar and I could try to climb the mountain, though none ever had, and traverse the ridge, though none ever would, and survive somehow in the land beyond. But it was too late for that as well, since the slope was slowly being covered in the sulfurous flow...trickles now, but soon rivers of lava would stream down its crags and folds, and the climb was already impossible for an elderly couple and their infant son.

It was then that love lit the way to a new path...the path of faith...the path to you.

I abandoned reason and begged the Firebird to save K'eL and take him out of the valley, over the ridge to your world. She was not big enough to carry us, but she would have just enough strength in her talons to fly the child aloft in a basket. We would wrap K'eL in a quilt that his mother had sewn for him. La'ar had embroidered it with the reds, yellows and blues of the Firebird, in tribute to our friend, and it would keep K'eL warm in the cold skies where the great bird soared.

The Firebird knew that if she left the valley, she would be leaving her nest behind her and, unable to return to it, she would never be reborn again. But she is drawn always towards love and so she agreed to take K'eL to find someone with love in their heart. The Firebird would fly over the mountain. She could do no less. From ashes she came and so to ashes she would return, as all things must...even a firebird.

La'ar and I wanted to savor every remaining minute of our lives with K'eL, so we kept him close to us a few days more, but I could feel the earth groaning, the mountain whispering to me as if to say, "run, run now," and that was when the Firebird returned. As I record these final thoughts, La'ar is now putting our child in the basket, so he may be flown to safety. And that is who you see before you now...our son, K'eL, born to us on the eve of our destruction and borne to you on the wings of the Firebird. We threw our child over a mountain and had faith that you would catch him. And so you have.

I do not know if you have magic in your realm, but K'eL is a child of magic. I suspect there is great power in his blood, even in a faraway land. In your world, a land where reason may prevail, magic will seem that much the greater, so raise him well and he may do wonders for you and your people.

All I ask is that you tell him of us one day...tell him that he had a mother and father who twice gave him life and we would be there with him if we could, and that he was the last son of the Krye'Dyn, a mighty but foolish people who invested their final hopes in him. Tell him we will live if he lives, and we will only perish with him.

The Firebird chose you because it is drawn always towards love. Your love will bring K'eL to your bosom and you will raise him as your own. I know this, for I am J'ol, seer of the Krye'Dyn, and I have seen the death of our people and our rebirth in your heart, rising up like a firebird.

Thank you, oh loving heart. Please kiss our child goodbye for us.

With boundless gratitude,
J'ol and La'ar of the Krye'Dyn

The woman, Klara, was moved by the letter—profoundly moved—but it was written by a madman, surely. She looked down at the ashes beneath the basket. They were laid out on the ground in the shape of a great bird. Well, the child was no less real for that and in no less need, whether he came to her at the hands of a madman or a mythical bird from a magical realm.

The sun was beginning to set and the sky was turning a deep crimson over the alpine mountains near Leonding. Klara took the sleeping infant, still wrapped in his multi-hued quilt, and placed him in her basket, atop the white edelweiss blooms. She headed home, excited and joyful and feeling younger than she had when she went up the mountain that day, but apprehensive, too.

Klara's husband, Alois, was a poor farmer of ill temper, but perhaps he would allow her to keep the boy. Edelweiss on the supper table always softened his disposition, just as its tea eased his digestion, and, besides, Alois knew the value of a son that could grow up and help work the land with him. The Austrian soil of Leonding required many hands to work it if their family was to pull a living out of the ground at this altitude.

And this boy, this K'eL (she would ask Alois to give him a good Bavarian name; she began to consider some), he would make a fine companion for their son, Adolph, who was sickly and small and stricken by dark moods.

Adolph could now grow up with this boy—this child from beyond the mountain—who might work miracles for his big brother one day.

She could not know whether K'eL's love would be enough to raise Adolph out of his darkness, or whether Adolph's nature would infect K'eL's spirit instead, but she had hope.

Yes, she had hope that one day her sons would be great men, *ubermenschen*, who would alter the course of the twentieth century now dawning, and together they would change the destiny of the world.

But all mothers hoped that for their sons, she supposed.

The Firebird
AUTHOR'S NOTE

Disclaimer: This is not a superman story. Any similarity to a superman story is...well, ok, it's intentional. But this story contains no copyrightable material created by DC/National periodicals, nor by their employees, contractors, indentured servants or successors in interest. Any similar elements contained herein are used only to evoke characters and situations so that they may be commented upon in this patently transformative work. Therefore, even if someone was drunk enough to claim this story somehow infringed something, this work falls safely within the scope of "fair use" defined under article 1.07 of the u.s. Copyright act [so the Time/Warner lawyers can go take a flying fuck at a rolling donut].

Superman is America's creation myth. A couple of Jews in Cleveland took the story of Moses and put him into the heartland of Depression-era America. They dispensed with God and, instead, gave their creation, their golem, all the power they could imagine and then sent him forth to take on injustice in all its guises. They created an immigrant whose fondest wish was to assimilate, so they gave him an alter-ego as a bumbling weakling and kept his true nature hidden from the world.

National Periodicals then bought Siegel & Shuster's invention for pennies, and they built an empire upon it, a mighty ziggurat, leaving the boys behind to slave away on the pyramid they themselves had designed, unacknowledged and woefully under-compensated until they were nearly gone. And if that isn't a summary of the American Dream, I don't know what is.

Siegel & Shuster built Superman on the standard SF motifs of the time, but it was SF thinly layered over religious allegory; its foundation was based on ancient myth. So, I've reconsidered the myth from a different perspective, using a different tone and structure to achieve a different purpose, stripping away the SF to expose the fantasy beneath.

"...if you do not understand why forty-seven samurai would march toward an unknown fate only to restore honor of their dead daimyo, then you are not understanding of Bushido, or the power of a story to live on in men's hearts, and nothing I say now will bring sudden comprehension."

Confessions of
the Last Ronin

US Naval Hospital
Saipan, Mariana Islands
Files of Dr. J. Loewen
August 12, 1975

Before rotating stateside, I make the
following report for the file regarding the
recently disappeared "Patient K".

K walked out of the jungle four days ago,
and was followed two days later by forty six
other Japanese men who, upon their arrival,
murdered an old man visiting from Tokyo.
Then they killed themselves, all of them

committing Hara-Kiri on the loading dock...except for K, who took no part in any of the violence.

After being taken into custody, K told and retold the most fantastic tale I've ever heard and, considering that I've been working in this psychiatric ward for seven years, I thought I'd heard them all.

K was in relatively good health, despite a hand scarred from a serious burn, and seemed otherwise rational. He wore a worn-out Japanese uniform circa WW II, as did the others, and one might think them all a group of "hold-outs"...those stragglers from the war that have popped up on these islands from time to time over the past thirty years. And if K, or any of them, were aged into their fifties, then that would make some sense. But K claimed to be seventeen years old and tests verified it. The bodies of the other soldiers were similarly youthful.

When I interviewed K, we had a stenographer present to record his narrative. So I present his story here verbatim [with a few parenthetically translated terms that have been included to clarify his statement]. But I must leave it to others to explain the tale of Patient K, since I cannot.

I will speak plainly to you, Dr. Loewen, as my English is not so elegant, and I am so wishing for you to understand.

As has been said, I am called Terasaka Kichiemon, born on this island of Saipan in the year 1927, as these things are reckoned by your calendar. Honorable father, Chuichi, left behind his life in Japan as *Kannushi* [Shinto priest] and became a sugarcane farmer here. Why he came to the island was never said. But having come, he fell in love with my sweet mother, Fu'una, a *Makhana* [shaman] of the native Chamorros.

Growing up in our village of Tanapag, I trained in the arcana of both their traditions and demonstrated unique adeptness in them. Mother often said that my talents were a gift from the gods, to keep me safe in a world unsafe for those born of two worlds.

Though spiritually strong, I was physically weak...because all magic has a price. Of little use in a sugarcane field or on a battlefield, I found my place tutoring the village children in languages and history. It was a suitable station for me, and the villagers, while never fully accepting of my mongrel status, at least let me be.

My parents had another child, a younger daughter. She was delicate, beautiful and the joy of our family. I do not remember her name. Why? Why can I not remember my own sister's name? She was only seven when war came to Saipan.

It was 13 June, 1944 when shelling started. The Americans were not expected so soon and island fortifications were not yet completed. But no amount of concrete would protect villages like Tanapag, nor our island's 25,000 Japanese men, women and children who wanted nothing more than to cut cane, eat a bowl of rice with their families, and pray to their ancestors for some dryer days and cooler breezes.

And so bombs fell for days, with shells raining on our island like a monsoon...flattening structures, tearing flesh, and deafening all to the point of insanity. Sister was killed when exploded burning metal fragments ricocheted wildly inside the cave in which we hid, coming to violent rest in her lovely face.

Finally, soldiers came. Wave after wave, Americans crawled out of the sea, scuttled over beaches and into the jungle, slaughtering everything in their way, leaving nothing alive in their wake...or so it was said.

They crept up from southern and western shores, so our family headed north, eventually trapping ourselves along the edge of the great cliffs at Saipan's northern point. There was nowhere else to turn and only the sea crashing against rocks so far below.

Meanwhile, as was later learned, Japanese forces were regrouping for a counter-attack. Those that spoke for the Emperor held private counsel with our generals, but as for civilians, there was but a single order: to throw ourselves off the cliffs rather than risk capture by western devils, with our Emperor's promise that we who died would have equal status in the afterlife with soldiers who perished in combat.

Already heartbroken by his daughter's fate, Father wanted to preserve our family's honor by jumping to his death, as thousands had already done, but Mother refused to permit it. She saw no honor in such an act; after all, the Emperor was not HER god. Yet Father was determined and, after giving me his sword and his *Omamori* [priest's pouch] he bowed to Mother and kissed her cheek. Then, without hesitation, he jumped. Mother, in shock, demanded my oath to hide in the jungle for as long as possible. She sent me away with a kiss and her Chamorro prayer stone, and then she followed her beloved down onto sea-pounded rocks.

Carrying sword, stone and pouch, along with my deep sadness, I journeyed south, toward Saipan's great mountain, Tapochau, which climbed skyward from the belly of the island. With my knowledge of terrain, I could hide up there until the heavens fell. But, as the gods would have it, I would not be hiding alone.

On my second night in the jungle, I saw what later was said to be Japan's last *banzai* charge on Saipan (in fact, it was not the last, but more will be spoken of that at a later time). Over 3,000 soldiers, followed by nearly 1,000 of our walking wounded, charged the Americans, swarming over enemy lines only to be pushed back by greater armament. But soldiers of Nippon continued on, hour after hour, on and on all through the night, throwing themselves at the Americans with no intention of surrendering, retreating or stopping until they were either victorious or dead. Those were their orders. That was a banzai charge.

I watched it from a hole beneath a fallen tree, undetected by death surrounding me, and sat in silent witness to limbs severed, heads blown apart, and boys blinded by flares, falling into pits of fire. I called upon all the gods I knew (and I know many) to ease suffering. But I do not think it helped.

The shooting stopped just before dawn. I climbed my way along hidden trails up into the bosom of the mountain, where one could secret oneself away, intending to wait out the Americans for as long as it may take.

It was then that I met Captain Oishi. He was leading a group of soldiers and civilians he picked up on his march to Tapochau, following a similar path to the one I had taken. But, with such a large band, Oishi was not as fortunate as I in avoiding conflict; he had lost many on his journey, and those that remained were exhausted, thirsty and hurt. That they had come this far armed only with pistols, swords and fortitude was nothing short of a miracle.

I proved of value to Oishi right away, showing him where could be found food and water, and where to hide from American planes which flew constantly overhead. There were other things known to me which would soon be of service to Oishi, but they were not spoken of then.

Oishi was a fine naval officer. I was told this by Oishi's loyal lieutenant, Kitani. A natural leader, Oishi was well liked and respected by his men. He set up camp in a sound location, established a perimeter, and assigned duties to all in his command. After a few nights, when the captain realized that his unit was not in immediate danger, he sat by a fire hidden from dangerous skies and shared with me a bottle of sake he had salvaged from a nearby village. And then he spoke of the tragic meeting of the generals.

Oishi and his unit were commanded by an admiral, the great Asano. Asano was a naval hero of Nippon, a descendent of a noble house whose ancestors were *daimyos* [lords] in the time of the shoguns, before deification of the Emperor. Oishi had fought by Asano's side since Manchuria and had come to love him, as did all who served with him.

Asano had Oishi accompany him to the meeting at the northern cliffs, near Marpi Point, where military leaders were debating their next move. General Saito, the ranking officer charged with the defense of Saipan, was an able commander but aged and infirm. His second, Colonel Kamei, a young Air Force officer with a glint of zeal behind his eyes, urged a banzai charge. Asano counseled against it, arguing that suicide would not help the Emperor achieve victory; what was necessary was a delaying strategy to draw out conflict long enough for the Navy to arrive with reinforcements. Saito was torn by indecision, but then a representative from the Emperor arrived, the advisor Kira.

Kira was not military, nor an elected official. He was, as Oishi explained to me with venom in his mouth, part of that class of men, "among them academics, philosophers, bureaucrats and sons-in-law," Oishi said, "who were pleased to have other men die for their grand ideas. They were parasites who risked nothing and so convinced greater men to risk all." I do not know of such things. I know only that this was said.

Kira insisted that General Saito order a banzai charge. The Emperor, as descendant and living embodiment of the supreme god Amaterasu, had proclaimed that our national honor demanded it, and he further ordered all civilians to kill themselves rather than turn their lives over to our enemies. When Asano asked to see such imperial orders in writing, Kira struck him sharply across the face. In defense of his commander, Oishi pulled his sword and launched himself at Kira, but Asano stopped Oishi, ordering him to attention. Asano again calmly asked of Kira to produce orders in writing, but Kira only turned away, ordering Saito to have Asano commit *Hara-kiri* for his cowardice. Kira departed, and how he left our island was not known, but Oishi was sure that he had, somehow. "That was the type of man Kira was," he said.

Saito ordered the banzai charge, but he was too ill to lead it so instead he would commit Hara-kiri before the charge began...and he ordered Asano to join him. As the admiral's second, Oishi was required to deal Asano the final blow, decapitating him after he disemboweled himself with a *Tanto* blade. Kamei would perform the same service for Saito and then leave to lead the charge.

Before the ceremony, Asano gave Oishi his final orders: he was to get as many men as he could to Tapochau, highest peak on the island, and stay alive and fighting until reinforcements arrived. And, if it was not offensive to his honor, would Oishi please to consider staying alive long enough to kill Kira? This charge Oishi accepted gladly, but with a heart made heavy by duty.

And so the generals died that day by their own hands, and thousands of soldiers who followed Colonel Kamei died with him upon American bayonets, and thousands of civilians died upon rocks below the northern cliffs at Marpi Point. And here was I, with Oishi's ragged band, somehow still alive. But how were we to stay that way?

The first weeks were most difficult. Americans made regular patrols around the mountain, with planes continuously flying low above us. Our group, over 150 souls to start, half soldiers and half civilians, struggled to work together. Some soldiers had followed Asano and Oishi since Manchuria, but others were from different units and different military branches. The civilians were mostly women, children and old men, all terrified and unused to military command.

But each night, Oishi would tell our makeshift brigade the story of Asano and Kira, reminding us of our orders, of our duty, and of our opportunity to reclaim honor.

As weeks turned into months, we abandoned one camp to establish another, and then we would circle back again, constantly out of our enemy's reach. I was Oishi's quartermaster and his map, identifying suitable trails and caves, and finding new sources of food and water...not a simple thing to do for a group this large. But I was determined to prove worth, whatever difficulties.

At each new encampment, I would fashion a crude wooden shrine in the Shinto manner, beneath a sacred tree and near a source of fresh water, as Father had instructed. Depending on need, either Omamori or Chamorro prayer stone was used to summon such *Kami* [spirits] as might be helpful to us. Oishi did not believe in such things of course, but he put up with my rituals because he assumed they gave me courage to do what was necessary. But his faith was not required, nor were the good graces of the soldiers...which was fortunate, since none was forthcoming.

After three months, our rice supply was dangerously low. I inquired if anyone had a jewel of any sort, perhaps a ring with a stone of some kind. As had become customary, my request was ignored. It was only nurse Aono, the lovely Aono, who responded to me, graciously offering her engagement ring. Since her husband and young son were butchered in the invasion, as she told me, she had no need of it any longer. She spoke of her tragedy not with the sadness one expected, but with an emptiness that was chilling.

I took the ring and put it in a boiling pot of water over a fire in front of the shrine, along with a scrap of paper from my pouch. I spoke words, words learned long ago, and danced around the fire.

Soon, a fox trotted into camp, curious and unafraid. Lieutenant Kitani ordered it shot for dinner, but I shouted a warning.

"No! That is a messenger from Inari, goddess of the harvest. Shoot her and we will surely go hungry!"

Kitani looked at me queerly but told Private Oba, who had raised his rifle, to hold his fire. The fox walked up to me, stared into my eyes, and then walked off into the jungle. I followed. She soon led me to a hidden cave behind a waterfall, housing a cache of rice and other supplies. Oishi was delighted with our discovery. Even Oba's broken leg, suffered when he fell while transporting supplies back to camp, could not dull Oishi's enthusiasm, though Oba's own good humor was understandably dampened. I cooked rice for Oba until he recovered, and we became friends. The others treated my rituals with respect thereafter.

Some months later, two scouts were shot in a skirmish with an American patrol. The Americans were held at bay by the indomitable Corporal Tanaka, allowing our wounded men time to be brought back to camp. But the Americans were likely to get past Tanaka at some point and would track the scouts back to us.

The men made it back, but were grievously and mortally wounded. At Oishi's request, I call upon Chamorro magic to safeguard the encampment. Using Mother's prayer stone, I summoned *Taotaomo'na*, unpredictable and violent spirits by nature. Upon their manifestation, they possessed the bodies of the dying soldiers, taking them without request or permission, and transformed the men into a stand of trees that blocked the path to camp.

When the Americans finally got past Tanaka, they slipped in among the trees, no doubt thinking that the grove would provide good cover as the soldiers prepared to open fire upon us. But the trees turned on the soldiers, whipping them with their branches, grabbing them with their roots, and pulling the men under the earth so quickly that they had no time to scream.

The trees served for many months as our guardians, and there they stood until the Americans burned them down with flamethrowers after we had encamped further up the mountain. When we returned, we discovered the charred ashes of the arbor, with bones of two soldiers lying among smoldering embers. I wept. I dreamt for many nights thereafter that I could hear trees crying out. But all magic has a price.

After that, Oishi moved me from the civilian compound to take up residence with soldiers. It was a gesture surely intended to bestow honor, but I knew what it was. I had become Oishi's sword and so he wanted me close at hand. And I was grateful for it, nonetheless.

More months passed before scouts discovered another unit heading our way. Oishi sent men to assess strength, location and course of enemy movement. Those sent high up the mountainside came down with frightening news. The American generals, undoubtedly irritated by our continued resistance, had sent a battalion to encircle Tapochau and sweep up its slope on all sides at once, creating an ever tightening noose to kill or capture any combatant in their path. No matter where we fled, they would discover us and we would be hopelessly outnumbered. Oishi turned to me. He said nothing, but his eyes gave orders and I obeyed.

I built a fire, boiled water, put in a prayer scrap from the pouch, and spoke sacred words. I asked Tanaka, our unit's best marksman, to bring down a bird, but Oishi would not permit it, fearing a gunshot would disclose our location to any nearby patrols. Tanaka just smiled, set aside his rifle and fetched his crudely crafted bow and arrows from his duffel. Tanaka was Yakuza; he could kill in so many ways that using a bow posed no particular obstacle. He brought down a dove with a single shaft. I poured its blood into the boiling pot, then spoke again the prayer...it became a chant and I wandered in the empty spaces between the words until they were heard by the spirit I sought.

This time, however, the spirit would not answer; dove's blood was not strong enough for a summoning of this kind. Sighing, knowing in my heart what must be done, I plunged my hand into the pot of boiling water, offering the gods my agony instead. They accepted my price. I stifled screams as best as possible.

Another dove flew into camp. It circled, and then landed on Oishi's shoulder. "It is an avatar of Hachiman, god of war and of samurai, Captain. He will show you the path," I whispered hoarsely, while coating my boiled hand with a numbing, healing salve of my own devising and wrapping it in a banana leaf.

The bird chirped its song and flew above us. Oishi watched it land on a narrow ledge on the mountainside, high above our camp. As the bird pecked at it, Oishi stared at the ledge. It was narrow but long, and well above the thick vegetation that formed a roof over the mountain trail.

Oishi summoned us--Corporal Tanaka, Lieutenant Kitani and me--to discuss his plan. "The American patrols always stay on the mountain paths...and they do not look up," Oishi said.

"They don't look up, Captain?" Kitani was confused.

"It is true," said Tanaka. "Whenever I track them, they look from side to side, and always down to avoid tangling their feet in the undergrowth, but not up, never up...until I kill them. Then sometimes they look up after they fall, but their eyes see nothing...*heh heh heh*." Tanaka always laughed when he spoke of killing Americans, and he had killed a great many of them. His laughter was a malicious rasp that cut to bone.

Oishi continued. "We will get everyone up on the ledge. If we make no sound, and if we are lucky, the enemy will pass us by. Once they pass, we'll be able to establish a new camp behind their lines, undetected. They will not soon sweep an area they have just cleared."

And so everyone got up on that ledge. Grandparents who could barely stand climbed up and stood silently upon it, holding hands with their grandchildren who strained against their own natures to be quiet and still. Wounded soldiers were held up there by their brothers in arms. Lieutenant Kitani made sure that Nurse Aono stood next to him. His affection for her was well known in the camp; it was sweet but sad, as her soul was too broken to return his love, but she tolerated his attentions anyway out of a gentle courtesy. And Oishi had me stand next to him, his well-trained hound at heel. Only Tanaka refused to take a place on the ledge.

"I have sworn to kill at least 100 Americans with my hands," grinned Tanaka. "I will not succeed by standing helplessly on a ledge. Good luck, Oishi." He grabbed a massive machine gun, meant to be fired only when mounted on a tripod, and slung it over his shoulder like a bamboo fishing pole. He lashed belts of ammunition across his broad tattooed chest, and tied a sash of grenades around his generous waist, with a revolver and a machete tucked into his bulging belt for good measure, and walked off into the jungle, with only his blood-freezing laugh left in his wake.

And so we waited. We waited on that ledge under a scalding Saipan sun, hour after hour, my hand throbbing in pain, until finally we saw them. The jungle was moving below us and we heard the tread of boots walking single file on the mountain trail. A roof of leaves covered the trail, but there were occasional patches left naked, leaving us exposed. But the soldiers never looked up. Still, it seemed inevitable that at least one of them would do so, if only to stretch his neck. That thought began to burrow into my brain like an earwig.

But before I accidentally willed such a thought into being, gunfire started. The burst of Tanaka's weapon was unmistakable, punctuated by exploding grenades and pops of pistol shots. The blasts came from the west, and the Americans took off running toward them without hesitation, leaving us behind and undiscovered.

In their rush to battle, their line passed us by. Soon enough we were behind them and so it was time to move. We came down off the ledge and attempted to rub stiffness out of legs. We gathered our few supplies and moved down the mountainside to find a suitable cave. After establishing a new camp, we waited every day for Tanaka to stroll in, smiling his deadly smile, with 100 American scalps in his belt. But he never returned. And I miss his laugh to this day.

We lived for many months thereafter without incident. We no longer had munitions to stage a serious conflict with the Americans, nor did opportunity present itself, since they had largely stopped patrolling the mountain. Even flyovers became rare. But each night, Oishi retold the story of Asano and Kira, Asano having become a hero out of legend and Kira a villain out of Hell. Oishi stirred the fire in our breasts, bonding us all in common purpose.

But one day a plane appeared low overhead. It dropped leaflets all over Tapochau, announcing that Japan would soon surrender and that no harm would come to us if we ceased hostilities and gave ourselves up. Oishi gave the paper no credit, but food was low, ammunition almost gone, and illness rampant. Something had to be done.

The captain ordered the civilians to surrender. Lacking military discipline, they refused to abandon their commander at first, but Oishi explained that their surrender would allow the remaining soldiers to stay in better fighting condition, not having to share limited supplies. And, as a smaller band, we could then move more quickly and easily. It was their civilian duty to support the soldiers, Oishi said, and so they finally agreed.

Oishi ordered Lieutenant Kitani to lead Nurse Aono and all the other civilians to surrender at the American detention camp near Tanapag. Kitani would never question an order, much less object to it, and the idea of being close to Aono for even a little while longer filled him with a quiet joy. Still, it was clear that Kitani was embarrassed to leave us before battle was over, and he was distraught by the sense of impending dishonor. He bowed to us before departing. Then Kitani, with Aono by his side, led the civilians out of camp and down the trail. We never saw either of them again.

Some weeks later, Oishi sent Private Oba to find out what had become of them. Oba found the refugee camp, and saw some of our civilians farming outside its fences. He managed to speak with one of them undetected. They were being well treated, the farmer said, but he was sorry to have to relate the fate of Kitani and Aono.

When Kitani surrendered the group to an American patrol at the base of Tapochau, Aono——sweet, broken Aono who had buried her soul in a cave with her husband and son——fired at the Americans with a pistol she had brought along for just that purpose. She killed three before being shot dead through her heart. Kitani ran to her fallen body and, gently cradling her head, kissed her lifeless lips softly for the first and last time. Then he put his pistol in his mouth and scattered his brains on a nearby banyan tree. He, too, had never intended to surrender but only to deliver the civilians safely, which he had done. Before being led to the refugee camp, the civilians insisted on burying Kitani and Aono right there on the trail, in a single grave. Their bodies might be there still. It is not known.

There were only forty-seven of us remaining, but it was enough. We started night raids again...killing guards, stealing supplies and weapons, and sabotaging equipment, with such Kami summoned to help as needed. But as many more months passed, we finally accepted the fact that naval reinforcements would not timely arrive, and that defeat was imminent, and that our mission was truly hopeless. Despair would have robbed us of our will if not for Oishi.

"My brothers, this is no time to rest. We are not yet done. Admiral Asano gave us orders that must be obeyed!" And again we heard the story of great Asano, and of insidious Kira who insulted his honor and caused his death. We were *samurai*, Oishi always reminded us, living in spirit of *Bushido* [the way of the samurai], and our daimyo had been murdered on our watch, rendering us *ronin* [masterless samurai], without honor. But if we killed Kira, we could enter the halls of our ancestors with honor restored.

It was nonsense, of course. We could not get off Saipan, much less all the way back to Tokyo, and even if we found our way there, Kira was the type of man who would keep himself safe behind high walls. Whether Japan rose or fell, Kira would always stay afloat, like a rootless lily pad, and would never leave himself vulnerable to some band of filthy, starving ronin. It was a doomed mission, but the story served its function, especially when the war itself seemed lost.

On those nights, Oishi asked what I could do, but I did not know how to be of use, ignorant as I was of any magicks that would transport us to

Kira, or Kira to us, while armies of the enemy and the sea itself stood in our way.

"If we wait long enough," mused Oishi, "the war will end and we might make our way home. Kira will someday forget all about Asano and will no longer be on guard...if he ever was to begin with."

"Perhaps, but we may have to wait a very, very long time," I replied, "and men are coming down with malaria and dysentery, and we are half-starving, with little rest, and living in a state of constant alarm. We might not last long enough to see your plan through, Captain, even if this war ended tomorrow."

"Think of something, Mr. Kichiemon. You are our last best hope." With that, Oishi strode off to bed.

And so I prayed, calling upon Omoikane, god of wisdom, and he came to me in a dream, as he sometimes did. "Call upon the sea dragon god," he advised, "and say to him 'Urashima Taro'." The name was unfamiliar to me, but Omoikane is not a god to ignore.

The next night, I went with Oishi and two riflemen, including my friend Oba, down the mountain, out toward the eastern sea, near the village of Hashigoru. When we arrived, we found a sea cave by the beach, out of sight. And so I began my ritual: building a fire, filling a pot and, when it was boiling, dropping into it the last remaining scrap from Father's pouch. I recited the summoning words, calling to Ryujin, dragon god of the sea, and chanted them until I entered that half-way place between words. Opening my eyes, I saw a man walk out of the surf.

Oba took aim but I put my hands on the rifle barrel, lowering it. "Ryujin comes," I whispered. No one knew what to make of that, but they stood warily aside as a god approached me.

"Mage, you summoned me." Ryujin's voice boomed with an echo of thunder.

"Yes, my lord."

"And what do you have the temerity to ask of me?"

"His lordship, Omoikane, told me to say to you 'Urashima Taro'."

Ryujin paused a while. "It is a difficult thing you ask of me."

"But I do not even know what it is that I have asked!" I admitted, confused.

The dragon lord laughed, and waves crashed in response. "How like Omoikane to send you forth unprepared." His laughter receded with the tide. "That old fool is suggesting that I perform a rare and dangerous magick for you, one that would bring an ageless sleep upon you and your comrades, a sleep from which you would awaken only when the sea was done with you."

I considered his words. Yes, that might work. In a few years, or perhaps only months, war would likely be over and we would be presumed dead. If the sleep is ageless, no time will have passed for us and we would still have just enough strength to make our way to Japan, find Kira, and restore Asano's honor...and so our own.

"But can even one as mighty as you do such a thing?" I queried.

"I've done it once before, for Omoikane's friend, Urashima Taro," he said. "All it requires is a mage of sufficient power to initiate the rite." He stared at me.

My eyes narrowed. "This sorcery...it is difficult, you say?"

"You seek to change the fundamental laws of the universe. So yes, quite difficult, and with results that might be quite...imprecise," he chuckled.

"Then it must surely come at a great cost."

At that, Ryujin shrugged his massive shoulders. Moonlight danced on his black hair like fireflies and amplified the shimmering phosphorescence of his scaly skin. He remained silent.

I spoke to Oishi. "Do you understand, Captain? Ryujin will allow us to journey forward to days yet to come, but how far a journey he cannot say. And it will be done at so great a price that even he dares not speak it. What shall we do?"

Oishi did not hesitate. "For honor, one must pay any price."

I paused. "Is it for honor, Captain, or for vengeance?"

"When victory is lost, vengeance IS honor. Do it, Mr. Kichiemon, whatever the cost." And that is how such things are decided.

Ryujin told me what must be done to initiate the rite and then he sighed—with what...bemusement, sadness, resignation? Most likely all that and more—and returned to the sea. We returned to camp.

Oishi discussed plans with his men. He would not order them to do this. They were free to surrender themselves and he would think no less of them. But if they would leave, they should step forward and go now. His men stood motionless, barely breathing much less willing to abandon their captain and their mission at this point in their lives. In the spirit of Bushido, they would follow him wherever he would lead. And if you do not understand why forty-seven samurai would march toward an unknown fate only to restore honor of their dead daimyo, then you are not understanding of Bushido, or the power of a story to live on in men's hearts, and nothing I say now will bring sudden comprehension.

We returned to the eastern beach. There I cast the last spell I would ever cast, reciting my last incantation, plunging both empty pouch and prayer stone into boiling water, and dancing my last dance on empty sands, white in the moonlight, as winds whipped around us and howled. I chanted words Ryujin gave me, entering for the last time that sacred space between words and worlds, until I found what I sought and brought it forth.

The sea raged, finally spewing forth a translucent bubble, coughed up by a creature so far below the waves that its existence could only be imagined. The sphere called to us with a siren's song that pulled us into it; we passed through its permeable surface and entered a world of beautiful light and sweet scented air, surrounded by the sound of soothing chimes. Exhaustion overtook us all and we fell where we stood, into a deep, contented sleep, as the bubble sank back beneath the sea.

And while I slept, I dreamt. I dream, *I am dreaming...*

I am dreaming of Ryujin's daughter, lovely Otohime. She gives me a small, empty wooden box.

"This box, called 'Tamatebako', will hold all the years that you and your companions do not age. But those years will come spilling out upon whoever opens it. So keep the box closed, sweet Kichiemon-Taro. Keep it closed forever,

lest you age violently and disappear into dust."

Then I dream of a great beast, Yamata Ni Orochi, an eight-headed dragon as big as Nippon itself, which was defeated long ago by the storm god Susanoo, son of Izanagi and Izanami, the first gods, creators of the world. Susanoo cast the dragon down to Earth's lowest depths, a trench at the bottom of the Marianas Sea from which nothing could escape. But in my dream, the dragon did escape; my spell had released him.

And so Orochi burst forth, its eight heads each spouting flames in all directions, its mighty tail poised to twirl the ocean into a maelstrom, its great talons prepared to rake Earth's tender flesh once more, with no storm god now to stop him. Was this the price of my spell, loosing this creature upon the world? The dream continued.

I could now hear a roar...a fearful roar of a great cat approaching. It was Byakko, the white tiger of the West, summoned down from its constellation in the night sky to stalk Orochi. The tiger was pale as the white peaks of Mt. Haku, its hide shiny and metallic, its teeth and claws sharp as Katana blades.

Where had Byakko come from? I knew no spell to summon him. Perhaps they had mages in the West, too, and they had sent forth their own beast to do battle. If so, they would be accountable for their own part in what was to come. As for me, I would have guilt enough to last until the end of days.

Byakko swiped his impossible paw and decapitated two of Orochi's eight heads. The dragon heads fell to Earth and, wherever their blood spilled, a poison mushroom grew and the land was devastated. One head fell upon the city of Father's birth, the industrial town of Hiroshima. The other fell upon the seaport city of Nagasaki, where Father served as a priest before coming to Saipan.

Two mushrooms sprout and two cities are consumed, and I hear screams... hundreds of thousands of people screaming while they burn, burn into ash, burn into vapor, burn into shadows on walls, mutilated with fire and poison that stays within them forever, even to be visited upon their children yet to come. The screams of generations of my people echo inside my head, endlessly. When would this dream, this nightmare be done? Was my sanity the price?

The screaming finally stopped when I awoke on the beach, alongside the others. It seemed like only a few minutes ago that we were stepping inside the bubble. Had Ryujin's spell failed? But no, the moon no longer hung above us, as night skies were dark with only distant stars in the firmament. And those stars were in the wrong place for this time of year.

We scrambled toward the cave, but as we approached we saw a new road, paved black, running along Saipan's old eastern trail. We hid behind brush in the dunes and watched. Vehicles traversed the black road, the cars and trucks dissimilar to those we knew. Beyond the road, we saw houses. They had not been here before; the huts of Hoshigoru were further north.

We ran back to Tapochau. We passed people near the houses...Japanese civilians, it appeared, but wearing western-style garb. And westerners were there, too, strolling through gardens, smiling at us and taking our pictures. None took any action against us; hostilities must have ceased some time ago.

We made it back to our cave. We found some of our belongings left behind. They were rotted, as if abandoned ages past. No one spoke for a long while.

Finally, Oichi asked me, "You read and speak English, Mr. Kichiemon, do you not?"

"Not perfectly but passably, Captain."

"I will write a letter. You will bring it to the Tanapag refugee camp and translate it for the American commander there."

"But they will not likely allow me to return with a reply."

"No. But if they accept our terms, they can send up a flare. We will see it."

"Yes, Captain."

I prepared to leave while waiting for Oishi to compose his letter. I said my goodbyes to Oba and the other men, who had all become my brothers during our time together, including the time spent sleeping beside each other in a bubble beneath the sea.

Oishi finished and handed me the document:

To the American Commander,

As the leader of combatants on Saipan in service to the Emperor of Nippon, I offer terms for our surrender to your authority.

I require only a guarantee of fair treatment for my men and the opportunity to turn my sword over to the Emperor's advisor, Kira, from whom my superior officer received his last orders and so remains the only one authorized to relieve me of my command.

Should these terms be acceptable to you, fire a flare toward Tapochau when Kira arrives on Saipan and we will turn ourselves over to you. If no flare is seen within three days, or if any harm comes to the courier of this letter, you may consider yourself at war with the forces under my command.

Honorably yours,
Captain Oishi
Commander of the Emperor's forces on Saipan

I read his letter, then folded it into my uniform jacket and bowed deeply to Oishi before walking off, northwest through the jungle, toward home.

The road to Tanapag was now paved and easier to travel than it had been when I last walked it with my family to Marpi Point. I arrived in no time, but there was no refugee compound anymore. There was only an American flag flying over this hospital where we now sit. So I came here, hoping to find someone in authority to whom I could entrust Oishi's letter.

You took me in, Dr. Loewen, treating me with kindness, for which I am grateful. You brought me to your Colonel, to whom I delivered and translated Oishi's terms. Surprised but amenable, he promised to accept Oishi's surrender and to bring Kira here, if he were alive and willing.

While waiting for Kira, I bathed, changed, and ate. Clean water, new clothes, fresh food…it was glorious! Later, you showed me a newspaper. It was dated 1975, thirty years since that night I last stood with Oishi on the sands of the eastern beach. Thirty years; I might have been surprised, but I was not.

You also showed me books that described the nuclear tragedy that ended the war. So my dreams were true, you see. I should have realized it sooner, of course, because my dreams have always been true, in one form or another. The books ascribed the blame as they may, but how could they understand the true nature of it? The books said, too, that the Emperor had survived the war, though he was forced to forsake his claim on godhood in the end. It was wise to have done so, I think, for when men become gods, all manner of misfortune follows.

Kira arrived. He was in his seventies, decrepit and not fully in control of his faculties. The Emperor ordered him to come and so he came, not sure at all what this was about. But he would soon learn the meaning of things.

The flare was fired that night. Oishi arrived the next day, leading his men to Tanapag in precise military formation. The Colonel invited me to accompany him and Kira, to meet the soldiers with an honor guard on the blacktop of the hospital's loading dock.

Oishi stepped forward, presenting his sword. Kira stepped forward, as instructed, to receive it. As they met, Oishi leaned forward and whispered, "I send you the greetings of Daimyo Asano, and in his honor I return to you the gift you once gave to him...the great gift of dying for the Emperor." Oishi stepped back and, with a quick stroke of his finely honed Katana, he sliced Kira in half, from the top of his head down to his genitalia, with both parts of Kira dropping to the tarmac with a sickening squish.

The Colonel and his guards were frozen in shock. Only I knew what was to follow. Oishi and his men screamed "BANZAI!", and the forty-six fell upon their swords. And so there they all were—Oishi, Oba, and the others, lying alongside Kira—and there I stood, Nippon's forty-seventh ronin, witness to the last banzai charge of the war, watching the blood of the dead, both honored and dishonored alike, pooling indiscriminately upon the black ground. And even after all that blood, I knew...I knew that the price was still not paid in full.

US Naval Hospital
Saipan, Mariana Islands
Files of Dr. J. Loewen
August 13, 1975

Regarding Patient K's disappearance, I conclude this report with a statement
by Seaman Emmett, the orderly I instructed to maintain around-the-clock
surveillance of K after the mass suicide.

Let it be noted that, after offering the following statement, Seaman Emmett
applied for medical furlough and will be returning with me to the States:

"I watched the guy through a two-way mirror as he sat in front of
a table in his room. He had all his stuff in a small sack, and he pulled
out of it a small wooden box. He looked up at the glass, staring at
me like he could see me through it, and he said:

'Megumi... my sister's name was Megumi. I remember it now.
It means 'Divine Grace'. Please, Mr. Emmett, tell Dr. Loewen that
for me.'

And then the guy opened the box..."

Confessions of The Last Ronin
AUTHOR'S NOTE

My father drove a tank in World War II, in the Philippines. When MacArthur said "I will return," he was not speaking of himself so much as he was of sending my dad and his buddies back into that malarial mosh pit of tedium and death.

Dad was a liberal-minded man, a Depression-era New Dealer, but after the war, when it came to the Japanese...well, I'll just say he took all their shooting at him very personally. And he was distinctly glad we dropped not one but two atomic bombs on them. Since he would've been one of the hundreds of thousands of men to land (and likely die) in the inevitable invasion of Japan had their Emperor not surrendered, I figured Dad had a right to feel as he did.

So when I started thinking about writing a war story, the war in the Pacific seemed the natural setting, and the dropping of the bomb the ultimate conclusion. But I had in mind to try and write it from the Japanese point of view, to voice my own particular ambivalence on the nuclear question.

When I came across the details of the Battle of Saipan in my research, and the true story of Captain Oba, a "hold out" who led forty-seven men out of Mount Tapochau six months after the war ended, I was reminded of *The Forty-Seven Ronin*, a historical incident which had evolved into a folk tale over the centuries, that has been adapted many times in many media. It's a uniquely Japanese tale of revenge and honor and loyalty and sacrifice, and the synchronicity of both stories dealing with the honor of forty-seven Japanese men in combat was too potent to pass up.

So I retained as many events from the Battle of Saipan and the activities of Captain Oba as possible, and merged them with the incidents and characters of *The Forty-Seven Ronin*, while blending in Shinto and Chamorro mythology, to make the magic of the story culturally inherent to the material.

Anyway, this one is for Dad.

"As the two sank down onto the coats and her lips
brushed against his, he finally understood. From now
on, there would be only this, just survivors in the
dark waiting for the storm to pass,
and nothing else mattered."

Survivors
in the Dark

Loewenstein would one day speak of his friend, Dr.
Franz Archibel, a colleague of his at the University
of Wisconsin at Madison. Here, Loewenstein offers
a brief anecdote that Dr. Archibel shared with him
over cocktails one rainy afternoon. Loewenstein
offered no assurances as to its accuracy, nor did
he guarantee the actual existence of Dr. Archibel,
or even of himself for that matter, but he views the
story's implication of a coming apocalypse as self-
evidently true.

-Editor

Y ou study... what?" she asked, licking
her lips hungrily.
"Cockroaches," Dr. Archibel
responded, sighing.

Bespectacled and slight, with thinning
hair and alarming pallor, Franz Archibel
was unaccustomed to being the object
of a woman's attention. Yet here he was,
at another cocktail party hosted by the
department chair's wife, but this time
surrounded by women—colleagues,
spouses, the catering staff—hanging on his
every word. And their eyes—some soft and

fluttery, others hard and carnivorous—all focused on him.

"*Periplaneta Americana*, of the order *Blattaria*. Modes of adaptation and reproduction are my speciality."

"Fascinating," said the woman, Mira, a smoldering brunette. "May I call you Archie?" she asked coyly, through those just moistened lips.

A pet name? From a beautiful girl? *Unprecedented*, he thought. "My name is Franz," he mumbled, stunned.

"You know, Archie, I find the scientific mind irresistible." Mira casually brushed back some strands of Archibel's limp hair. Her touch sent an electrical charge through his body.

"Yes, thank you, I mean...what was I talking about?"

"Reproduction," said the waitress, passing by with a tray of crab cakes, her mouth curled in a secret smile.

"Please, professor, don't talk about reproduction," urged Emily Samsa, the hostess. Carrying triplet girls *en utero* made Emily sensitive to the subject. "Every woman I know is pregnant." Her guests laughed.

"But it's fascinating," continued Archibel. "The cockroach has been with us since before the dinosaurs."

As he spoke, a woman across the room rocked a pink-blanketed infant in her arms. Babies seemed to abound these days, he observed. What was he saying?

"Um...but...how did they survive the cataclysms that brought so many other species to extinction? Adaptation! The cockroach, you see, is—"

Emily sidled up to him and whispered, "Franz, this is why you always leave these parties alone, despite my best efforts and the diminishing supply of eligible men. Talk about something else...the odd weather, anything!"

Mira, however, continued to show intense interest. "But what does your work have to do with, you know, people?" She was unconsciously spooning too much sugar into her coffee. Franz pretended not to notice.

"You would be surprised by the amount of genetic material humans have in common with insects, especially ones that have been swimming in the gene pool for three hundred million years. In fact, a recent experiment

I conducted may have profound implic—"

Franz was interrupted by Dr. Upson Samsa, the host and his department chair, handing him a Bloody Mary. "Emily thought you could use this...oh, I see you've met Mira; she's my new assistant. Mira, I'm afraid Dr. Archibel here is a confirmed bachelor, so go easy on him." Samsa chuckled and wandered off. Archibel flushed.

"Please Archie, continue," coaxed Mira, nearly purring.

"Oh, what was I...oh, yes. Profound implications..."

"Franz, hold Dottie a moment, I need to pee." Professor Berenbaum pushed her toddler into Archibel's arms, causing him to spill his drink down his white linen pants. Berenbaum disappeared down the hall. Dot hugged Archibel tightly.

"You have a way with children," observed Mira.

"Not really," Franz replied, shocked.

"Are roaches good parents, too?" she teased.

"Yes, surprisingly maternal."

"What's surprising is that they're able to attract mates at all since they look like, you know, cockroaches," Mira giggled and then went wide-eyed, seemingly shocked by the sound.

"Yes, I see what you mean. Ha." Archibel put Dottie down so he could clean off his trousers. She hugged his leg like it was her Build-A-Bear.

"Actually, not all roaches try to attract mates. There's a rare strain that reproduces through parthenogenesis."

"Partha—?"

"*Parthenogenesis*. Asexual reproduction."

"Asexual? Well, that doesn't sound like any fun at all!" Mira tried to help Franz by wiping his crotch with the napkin in her hand.

"So that was your profound new discovery?" she continued, nonchalantly, as she stroked his groin.

"Um...what...oh, no. That's fairly old news...please, thank you, I've got it." Archibel took the napkin from her and started wiping himself.

"I recently altered their environment so radically that this particular intrusion of roaches should have eventually died out. But, instead, the females started breeding at a tremendous rate, disgorging a disproportionately large number of female progeny. The environmental impact did cause a precipitous decline in the male population, but enough males remained to keep the female population, um, populated."

"How terribly sexy," Mira whispered.

"My theory is that it's a genetic failsafe, hardwired. When faced with extinction, the female overbreeds the species to survival. Amazing, really."

Franz had succeeded in spreading the tomato juice further down his trousers.

Berenbaum came back and peeled her daughter off of Archibel's leg. "Oh, did Dottie do that?" indicating the stain. She reached for a napkin. "Let me get that for y—"

"Yes, I'll just go back there and take care of this myself, thank you both."

Archibel retreated to a guestroom down the hall. He sat on the edge of a bed piled with coats, the only light in the room coming from a TV droning on in the corner. Fox News was bleating at him, with talking heads shouting about whether the continuous warnings of imminent natural disasters on a scale that would make Noah weep was just more liberal junk science or whether it marked the "end of days" as described in the *Book of Revelation*.

There was a soft knock at the door. Mira entered the darkened room, unbuttoning her blouse as she crossed to him. Franz froze. As the two sank down onto the coats and her lips brushed against his, he finally understood. From now on, there would be only this, just survivors in the dark waiting for the storm to pass, and nothing else mattered.

The upside of the gradually encroaching apocalypse was that even males like him wouldn't have to be alone anymore, and so his life-long terror abated. In fact, there was only one thing for him to be afraid of ever again...

...*Parthenogenesis*.

Survivors in the Dark

Author's Note

I had just finished writing the lengthy "Mad Gilly" western and I needed to see if I could write something short, which is harder than it sounds. I had in mind a piece of "flash fiction"—a short-short story of under a thousand words. Since I had been fooling around with a notion that seemed right for that length, I took a shot.

My wife and I had once been to a barbeque with a bunch of my old college buddies and we noticed that many of us had just started having kids. Since most of us were in our early thirties at that time, it was not a bizarre occurrence to note. What was odd, though, was that almost all of the kids happened to be girls. And I remember thinking: *it must be the end of the world, with our womenfolk trying to breed enough females to keep the species alive*, or some notion that was similarly unevolved.

After deciding to turn this into a story of some sort, I started doing some entomological research into species that could spontaneously breed to survive, and I discovered cockroaches. I don't like to think about cockroaches, but there I was, thinking about cockroaches. I used character names from various bug-based stories (purely for my own amusement) to tell the story of a nerd who finally gets laid at the end of the world, because that's apparently what it would take. And I tell it against a backdrop of the apocalyptic "climate change" issues of our time.

The story is probably a reflection of my ongoing amazement that a woman like my wife ever agreed to date me, much less marry me. The generosity (and bad judgment) of women never ceases to astound and is the single best reason our species perseveres.

The webzine *Everyday Fiction* took a liking to the story and, after I did some further rewrites to clarify its apocalyptic premise, they published it in April, 2014.

"But what ill-intentioned hand would be moved to encapsulate eldritch devotions to a goddess of war and chaos? I must go back to the book and stop wasting my time with the others in the index. They are merely shadows on the cave wall; Morrigan's Grimoire is the fire."

Gods
Out of Time

"15 March–
Loewenstein,
She is coming. I will do what I can to stay her
progress, but I may fail. It is likely I will. In
which case, goodbye, dear Joseph.

-Wingate"

On the dusty shelves of the Mysticonic University Library, between the weathered volumes of the *Liber Ivons* and the *Necronomicon*, sat a book which would later be identified as *The Morrigan's Grimoire*. The ancient tome gave the impression that it had been laying undisturbed for centuries, but in fact it had just suddenly appeared among the library's holdings, apparently out of nowhere. Mysticonic's chief librarian, Danforth, wrote to my dear friend, Professor Nathaniel Ephraim Wingate, the world's pre-eminent scholar in Proto-Celtic languages, requesting that he come to authenticate the book and translate it before it vanished again.

Wingate was my colleague at the University of Wisconsin at Madison, and though our scholarly pursuits overlapped only but a little, I had great affection for the old man and deep respect for his enthusiasms, not to mention his brilliance, unparalleled in his field. He also maintained a cabinet of fine brandies, and always had a cigarette case filled with Dunhills on his desk from which I emancipated cigarettes from time to time, when Winnie wasn't looking.

If that wasn't enough, he was also a master of two-handed Whist, and it was over one such game that Winnie told me of this sudden opportunity.

"Yes, of course I have doubts about the book's authenticity, Joseph, but I shall keep a precise log of my activities in my journal, so even if the book itself proved fraudulent, the process of working on it, and having access to Mysticonic's legendary private collection, will at least provide me with grist for a new article. Publish or perish, you know."

Indeed I did, but I preferred he didn't do both.

"But you will keep me posted, yes?" I asked, not really intending it as a question. I played the king of hearts and lit a stolen Dunhill.

"Oh, you worry like a mother hen," he cackled, trumping my king and winning yet another trick.

Winnie was surprisingly vital and robust for a man of his advanced years, but he would be spending long hours working in the unheated catacombs of a stone castle that was probably as old as the commonwealth in which it was situated. It was an activity which would tax a man half his age. And so, yes, I was concerned for him.

But the old man wouldn't use phones (much less e-mail, or most any other modern technologies) and he expected to be gone for months, perhaps even through the end of the upcoming school year, so he promised to post a letter to me from time to time to keep me apprised of his situation. I could look forward, then, to receiving his notes; they would be embroidered with that same elegant cursive with which he filled those leather-bound journals he loved to use.

And so I received his letters for the next six months and they gave me some relief...at first. But the tone of his correspondence changed over that time to indicate a mind buckling under increasing strain, deteriorating as the leaves turned and the snows came, and his final note to me was so dire that I determined to investigate his situation myself.

It was mid-March when I arrived at the university, and the lion of winter still held Mysticonic in its lacerating claws. Librarian Danforth's greeting was likewise chilly.

"Professor Wingate is no longer here, Dr. Loewenstein. He suffered a mental breakdown of some sort; students found him naked in the snow, trying to climb the statue of King Arthur that stands out in the quad. The authorities whisked him away to the Sefton Asylum."

My god, an asylum...oh, dear Winnie.

Sefton was some hundred miles or so north. I called there immediately and spoke to a doctor, a fellow named Mannerbund.

"We're still running tests, but no, we don't understand his condition yet, and your friend remains comatose and unresponsive. But, if you're coming, could you please bring his belongings up from the university?"

I told the doctor I would, but an ice storm had settled over Mysticonic and no one would be going anywhere anytime soon.

"I'd appreciate a call if there is any change in his condition," I said, and he promised he would let me know.

I returned to the library to ask Danforth for more details, but he had little to offer. At my request, he led me to the room in which Winnie had been working.

"The professor actually started living in here; he moved his things from the faculty quarters," Danforth reported.

The room was furnished as if by a monk who thought monks lived too extravagantly and so was determined to make his life an ascetic counterweight. A windowless chamber, the room was lit only by candles, some of which had burned down into hard white puddles on a ramshackle desk in the corner. Danforth lit one on the wall by the door. Through the dim light, I could make out a swayback cot across the room, with Winnie's suitcase lying open beneath its worn-out springs serving as his only dresser. Next to the cot was a small nightstand, unsteady on its feet. On it stood a candlestick, next to Winnie's cigarette case and lighter, with two of his journals lying beside them.

Whatever notations the journals contained, they were not the only repository of his writing in that room. The limestone wall nearest his bed was replete with symbols drawn onto its rough surface with an ochre paint of some sort, wielded by a hand increasingly shaky and unsure. The drawings were unfamiliar to me, even though I was not entirely ignorant of Winnie's field of study, and left me feeling somehow unsettled.

"We found him squatting naked on his cot, using the blood from his palms to write on the wall," said Danforth. "We called in security to remove him to Sefton. He escaped and ran amok through the campus."

Wingate "ran amok"? Impossible, I would have thought. But apparently I would have been mistaken. Maybe there was something here that could provide an explanation.

"Would you mind leaving me for a bit, Mr. Danforth?"

"Certainly, doctor. Just let the staff know if you require anything." He spun on his heels and departed, closing the heavy chamber door behind him.

With the storm still raging and with nowhere else to go, I used Winnie's Zippo to light the bedside candle. I sat on his cot and picked up one of the journals off the nightstand, then opened it to the last page and read the final entry:

"*14 March –*

All is not what it seems. I can feel the creature stirring. She is coming. Can I stop her? How? My blood is tainted, and my codex is missing. I will write to Loewenstein. He must know of this. Everyone must know. But perhaps it is too late, and I'm just a fool. Perhaps I should just say goodbye."

Disconcerting, to say the least. I would have to read his notes from the beginning to learn how my friend was brought to such a state of utter dislocation and then, perhaps, find a way for him to return from the nightmare to which he had been consigned.

The first journal began:

"*30 September –*

I have arrived at Mysticonic, a small, frozen college town in Rhode Island. The university is charming—old world, with ivy-covered walls and such. But the library itself feels out of place, as if from another time. A massive stone structure, with flying buttresses holding up its high vaulted ceiling, it was like some medieval church or castle from 1,500 years ago, similar to those I recall from my youth in Wales. It is a faux construction, naturally, or perhaps they shipped it over stone by stone from Tintagel? Regardless, it stands apart.

I will visit Danforth there tomorrow. Today, I settle in to the lodgings reserved for visiting faculty. The accommodations are modern and charmless, but are quite sufficient."

"*2 October –*

I met yesterday with Danforth, the head librarian, and he is a queer duck, as odd as the library itself. Tall, bony, bald and bespectacled, he is overly solicitous, unctuous even, yet wary of my attentions to anything but the object of my visit. There were other librarians and faculty scuttling about, and students too, of course, but they paid us no heed.

Danforth led me to the archives. We walked down a narrow corridor that ended with a large ouken door marked with a strange and unfamiliar design. He unlocked it with a key he had tied about his neck and we proceeded down a spiral stone staircase lit by candle sconces, down to a subterranean storehouse.

It was dark and cool down there, and surprisingly dry. They must regulate the heat and humidity carefully, to preserve their priceless assemblage of writings going back to papyrus scrolls from Egypt and even older Akkadian tablets. Certainly there was no direct light or dampness present to expedite deterioration. Well done, Danforth.

We wandered through stygian tunnels that seemed to go on forever in the flickering light, coming finally to a wrought-iron gate decorated with the same odd pattern as on the wooden door upstairs [I must examine that sigil more closely, at some point]. Danforth's key opened the gate and we entered the inner sanctum...the 'private collection', as it is known in scholarly circles.

The walls were lined with artifacts for as far as my eyes could reach through the shadows. My heart began to race as I examined the treasure trove of antiquarian objects and documents unrivaled anywhere in the world since the fires in Alexandria. And now it shall be mine for as long as I may require. This may prove to be the pinnacle of my long career.

I was lightheaded for a moment, but after I reoriented myself, Danforth revealed the thing for which I had come...the book. I donned thin cotton gloves and examined it. I could see the signs of advanced age along its split binding and its brittle leather cover. The book would be easily damaged and might even crumble if not carefully handled. I laid it on a table and opened it gently. Through the gloves, I could feel the embossing of the calligraphy on its browning pages. And then I felt a sudden chill that penetrated me to my very core.

I have always loved the smell of old books, with their musty, wood-based natural decay in a state of constant tension with the inks, covers, and binding that work to slow its inevitable disintegration. Books are living things. They are organic sandcastles built by the sea, waiting for the inevitable tide to wash them away, so we must experience their beauty before they vanish. I cannot comprehend those who choose, instead, to commune with little zeroes and ones on electronic devices and consign to civilization's scrap heap this experience with life.

This book feels different to me, though; its relationship is not with life but with its inevitable conclusion. It gives me a sense of foreboding, yet my dread stands upon a rampart of thrilling anticipation.

But that is enough for today. Loewenstein would not want me to overextend myself."

"10 October –

*I grow increasingly frustrated. These 'Celtic runes', as Danforth
called them, are not runes at all, of course. Runes are not used in Celtic
writings; they are originally Nordic, later adopted by Germanic tribes.*

*But these symbols represent no specific alphabetic structure, nor any
known system of glyphs or sounds or words or phrases that I can now
decipher. Their style precedes Celtic; they likely arose before runic systems
came to the British Isles with the Vikings and later the Saxons, before
even the pictographs and hieroglyphs of the ancient world. They comprise
a unique language that contains elements of each of these, and is evocative
of them, yet predates them all."*

"16 October –

*Progress, finally. Progress seemingly out of nowhere. The book is
entitled* The Morrigan's Grimoire, *and I have come to learn this in a
dream. I think my unconscious mind has grown tired of my daily failures
and has taken the horse by the reins, as it were. And so I have stumbled
upon the translation in my sleep and have awoken knowing.*

*It was in the shadowlands of my imagining where I saw symbols on
the book's cover arrange themselves into that unfamiliar appellation...*
The Morrigan's Grimoire. *I will research the title in the private
collection's index and see what there is to see about that."*

"23 October –

*Though it is well organised, the index provides damnably little. A
'grimoire' refers to any book of magic (spells, incantations, and the like)
and there are examples of such going back to antiquity, including some
here in the private collection.*

*And 'Morrigan'? That name belongs to any number of entities,
both historical and mythological. But based on the style of the book's
construction and its apparent age, it may be referring to the ancient Irish
war goddess, The Morrigan. I must write of this to Loewenstein; Celtic*

and Brythonic myths and legends are within his area of expertise.

But what ill-intentioned hand would be moved to encapsulate eldritch devotions to a goddess of war and chaos? I must go back to the book and stop wasting my time with the others in the index. They are merely shadows on the cave wall; Morrigan's Grimoire is the fire."

"31 October –

All Hallows' Eve. Students are likely roaming about in the cold, getting into all sorts of mischief. But in Wales, it is 'Nos Galan Gaeaf', the night before the first day of winter and, according to the lore of my Druid ancestors, it is the night that spirits wander the world. As has been my custom on this evening since childhood, I cut some ivy from the wall outside and placed ten leaves beneath my pillow. That should preserve me against such bogeymen as may tonight be scampering about this haunted place.

As to the book, after that breakthrough with its title, I thought my continuing efforts would yield immediate results. But the Grimoire is not so easily mastered. Just when I think I have found the book's Rosetta Stone, the symbols reorganise themselves.

I spend my days studying and noting its ever-changing patterns in a separate journal, creating a codex, and thus leaving this one to record my thoughts and feelings alone. My drawings in the codex are as undecipherable as the Grimoire itself, but I believe that this re-creation of the symbols in my own hand, accompanied by my contemporaneous annotations, will be the key to greater understanding."

"4 November –

It has been three days since All Hallows' Eve and I can only now bring myself to record my thoughts about it. The ivy clearly failed me that night. While asleep, dreams came. No, not dreams...visions. And not just visions...a voice. I heard a voice narrating the story that I had been staring at for the past month within the pages of the Grimoire.

And now I record the voice's words here, since I can somehow still *hear each syllable echoing in my mind:*

    'I am Blaise, the last scribe of the fallen King Vortigern of the Britons, and for posterity I write within this ancient book of signs and secrets the story of the king's grandchild, the cambion called Myrddin Emrys. And I write of the dragon beneath the tower, and the coming of the green man of the wood, and the Druid sacrifice within the great circle.

    It is a tale told in the name of The Morrigan—she who shall return one day to herald the coming of Graale, the dark god who lives beyond the stars, who came into being before all the other gods that followed thereafter...Graale, the first and the last, the alpha and omega, the maker and destroyer of worlds.'"

"7 November –

I dreamed of Graale that first night, after the book spoke to me...a tentacled creature undulating in the blackness of space, its single eye a bottomless black orb with a red corona, its massive maw, crusted with cilia, large enough to swallow worlds. It was cold fury and relentless hunger, a nightmare from which I awoke in a cold sweat.

Now, some days later, the voice has returned.

    'Myrddin Emrys was borne of the unholy union of a demon incubus with Princess Adhan, King Vortigern's daughter, who laid with the demon in her nightmares. The king looked upon Adhan's half-breed issue, a cambion, and saw that the newborn was hirsute and misshapen as it suckled at its mother's breast. He would have had the corrupted child thrown from the parapets of Carmathen Castle, but was advised by his Druid priest, Gwenc'hlan, that his grandson would prove of great worth one day. So, instead, the king sent his daughter and her misbegotten offspring up to the tower, where they would be locked away and out of sight from the world until need required their return.

Upon his tenth birthday, Myrddin, no longer ugly but instead seemingly human in aspect, was sent from the tower by Vortigern, torn from his mother's side to live in the nearby forest of Brocéliande, so he might learn the ways of the Druids residing therein.'"

"10 November –

My sleep has been troubled, fearing a return of my nightmare. I nap off and on, on a cot I had Danforth bring into this room which I have taken as my office. The Grimoire called to me constantly from the catacombs of the private collection, so I had it removed here, to this room. But now, when I hear the voice, I cannot always tell whether I am asleep or awake.

'In Brocéliande, Myrddin spent many years learning how to shift his shape from one living form to another, and how to master the Druid secrets of twig and flower and root and vine that would enable him to sacrifice the life of the world to create spells of great power.

And it was in Brocéliande that Myrddin first learned of the gods—gods like The Morrigan, whose destiny it was to one day summon Graale, a monstrous being older than any in the universe...Graale, who would stand against the One God that was first brought to this isle by our Roman conquerors. The invaders were now departing after centuries of occupation, back to their native lands at the call of their Christ, but they planted their One God in our fertile soil and it has taken root.'"

"13 November –

The words of Blaise burn through me now like an endless river of flame. The voice weakens me, degrades me, uses me up. I feel out of control. Oh, what I wouldn't give to be sharing a pleasant game of Whist and a snifter of Courvoisier with Joseph right now. Damn it, I would even

*let him steal my cigarettes and pretend not to notice. But, instead, I open
the book once more, for it now leaves me no other choice.*

'Upon the retreat of the Romans, the savage Saxons, led
by the twin demi-god warlords, Hengist and Horsa, had taken
the lands to the north and east and would soon try to fight
their way west to Briton, intent upon taking the head of King
Vortigern.

Though the king had a mighty fortress to defend his
border, Dinas Emir, its great tower had grown unstable.
Each day it would be repaired and each night rumbling from
below would cause it to fall anew. The king's Druid priest,
Gwenc'hlan, advised Vortigern that a dragon stirred beneath
the tower of Dinas Emir, awakened by the desecrating
presence of Saxon deities in the land. If it awoke, horrors
would follow and none would be spared. Even if it did not rise,
its continuing disquietude would bring the fortress down and
leave them helpless before the Saxon horde.

A sacrifice would be needed to save the tower. The blood
of an unfathered boy would have to be sprinkled on its
ground to silence the restless beast below. And so Vortigern
summoned Myrddin, a half-demon spawned by no man, to
return from Brocéliande so that he may be properly slain and
bled.

Vortigern's soldiers were sent to escort Myrddin to Dinas
Emir under some pretext, but the young wizard had grown
too powerful to be so easily ensnared. He transformed into a
great bird and escaped, then stole his mother, Adhan, from the
king's castle keep, carrying her off to distant Salisbury, as he
was advised to do by his teacher, Gwenc'hlan...the king's own
Druid advisor, with an agenda all his own.

On that desolate plain there stood the cromlech known
as Stonehenge, a great circle of cyclopean stones which had
been brought to that place ages past by The Morrigan herself.

Only there could Myrddin summon the goddess to deliver the tyrant king to his enemies for their pleasure.'

I closed the book. My head throbs; I can feel the blood pulsing in my veins. I must rest now, whatever dreams may come."

"27 November –

The students of Mysticonic are mostly absent; it is Thanksgiving in New England and even Danforth has flown from this place. I assumed he had no home to return to beyond the walls of this shadowy structure, and no family other than the crows that flew above the parapets, though I suppose even Danforth has a nest somewhere.

But I do not.

I have studied my genealogy for decades, tracing it back to the ancient Wales being described in the Grimoire, and I am the last living descendent of my line. Perhaps this is why the book resonates for me so, drawing from me a palpably physical response, stabbing me with pangs of the familiar even within its ghastly otherness.

I must learn of Myrddin's fate and I cannot be bothered with petty distractions any longer. I have moved all my things into this room and so now I can labour and sleep, as need be, in proximity to the book that lives here beside me...and within me."

"3 December –

'Myrddin gazed upon his mother, as she sat upon a rock at the centre of the great circle. Her mind had long ago fled the awfulness of her life and her shell was all that remained. But this may have been a blessing from the gods, so as to spare her from any awareness of what was to come.

A sacrifice was needed to summon The Morrigan, and the most potent offering is the life of an innocent when transmogrified by flame. Thus the Druids came to Stonehenge that night, the night of the winter solstice. This was Gwenc'hlan's plan...to use both Adhan and her cambion child to raise The

Morrigan and have her blow the summoning horn. This would herald the coming of Graale into the realm, for it was only that dark force that could drive out the One God that now infected Briton and was destroying the natural order. All were pawns in Gwenc'hlan's greater game, and now the sun and moon were aligned and the time was ripe. A fire had to be lit to waken the gods.

The Druids built a man within the great circle—a giant man of straw and vine, a wicker man, and into it they bound the docile Adhan. Myrddin, finally realizing the jeopardy into which he had placed her, attempted to thwart the priests and save his mother, but they entranced him and laid him down upon the circle's altar stone. As he laid there, helpless, they carved the summoning symbols into his very flesh, slicing him carefully with the legendary Dragonsword, a blade made by The Morrigan herself, forged in dragon's fire and tempered in dragon's blood. In this way, they could prepare Myrddin's body to be a doorway through which the goddess could emerge.'

I recognise the sigils being etched into Myrddin's body; I can see them in my mind's eye. They include those I've drawn in my codex, though their meaning still remains beyond my understanding.

'Vortigern had dispatched his soldiers to follow the Druids to the Salisbury plains, determined to retrieve Myrddin, and Adhan, too. The king's commander saw the flames of the wicker man in the distance and could smell the familiar odor of burning flesh wafting on the foul wind. He led the phalanx across the plains to the great circle. They were too late for Adhan, yet Myrddin was still within their reach.

But the Druids had finished their ritual. Myrddin's body glowed and floated a foot above the altar stone; his eyes rolled back and then an explosion of white light erupted through his violated skin, up into the midnight firmament.

Out of that effulgence strode The Morrigan, a mighty

Valkyrie with flaming red hair, standing one hundred yards high, with a fiarlann spear in her hand and the great battle horn of Graale at her hip. A murder of crows circled above her as the warrior goddess stepped out of the great circle. She crushed the king's army beneath her booted heel and slashed them with her edged spear, all the while laughing a laugh of noisome delight.'"

"24 December –

I have not been able to translate my recent thoughts into words on paper. The events I transcribed on that night three weeks ago still haunt me and I cannot escape them in my dreams, but perhaps they can be exorcised through my ruminations here.

It is Christmas Eve, and mayhap the Christian god will have mercy on me tonight, since the gods of my ancestral land precede any notions of mercy or compassion. But gods, whether Christian or pagan, cannot be counted upon. I must discover for myself the means to combat this possession of my mind before I am driven out of it.

'The Druids had sought to bind The Morrigan to their purpose but, once summoned, the goddess was beyond all human control. After annihilating the last of Vortigern's army, she turned and began plucking up the Druids...and devoured them, each in turn. She relished the crunch of their bones in her mouth, luxuriated in their death cries, savored their flesh succulently seasoned with terror, and then, after wiping the viscera from her chin, she grabbed up another of them, and then another, as they attempted to scurry away.

Seeing this, the panicked Gwenc'hlan made his way back to the altar stone. To break the spell, he plunged the Dragonsword deep into Myrddin's heart. Myrddin screamed and his shriek was echoed by The Morrigan.

'No! Not yet!' the goddess bellowed. 'I must blow the horn to summon...' Her words trailed off as she faded back into the light from whence she came, disappearing back through the bleeding fissures that marked Myrddin's desecrated body.'"

"25 December –

Christmas Day. Church bells chime to commemorate the birth of the Christ. He would later rise after his death, but he was not the only one to have done so.

'Despite the mortal wound inflicted by Gwenc'hlan, Myrddin did not die. Cambions cannot be so easily destroyed. Instead, he awoke screaming, and he remembered all that had transpired and could feel the monster that now resided within him. He saw the smoky ash of the wicker man, his mother incinerated within it, and the gory remains of the priests and soldiers, crushed and masticated, their entrails scattered about the Salisbury plains, rendered a charnel house by the goddess's fury. And in that moment, Myrddin went utterly and completely mad.

The Druids had used the Dragonsword to carve his flesh and so, having tasted his demonic blood during the ritual, the sword now connected to him and could not kill him. Myrddin pulled it out of his chest and severed the whimpering Gwenc'hlan's head with a single swipe. He determined then to disappear into the western forest, but ere he fled, he drove the sword deep into the altar stone, all the way to its hilt, so no one else could ever conjure its power.'"

"29 December –

Christmas passed without further incident. The campus is quiet over the holidays, buried beneath ceaseless snows. The students and staff have mostly returned to their homes to celebrate...

'...to celebrate a false and stolen day, the day of Alban Arthuan, the winter solstice, when the Druids honored the Mother Goddess with a burning Yula, and decorated a great pine, a Yule tree, with symbols of the sun, the moon, the stars, and the souls of those who had died, and with little gifts offered to the gods. But now the ritual of the Yula has been appropriated by the One God, and where its flame once represented the rebirth of the sun, the day has been corrupted so to honor the birth of the son, instead.'

Those words are not mine. They came out of me from the voice in my head. Myrddin's madness has infected me along with him."

That was Wingate's last entry in the journal. But before I had time to pick up the next one and follow his odyssey further, Danforth arrived with a tray of food. I was hungry, but the intrusion was unwelcome.

"How are you faring, Dr. Loewenstein? Any progress? Have you broken the code?"

"I don't have the skills to break the code, Mr. Danforth. Only Wingate did...does. And you saw the toll it took on him."

I turned away and reached for the second volume. I was suddenly aware of the absence of the third journal, the one Winnie had described as the codex, containing his notes on each of the specific symbols that he had reproduced on its pages.

"Did you take one of Wingate's journals, Mr. Danforth?" I queried.

"Yes."

"May I ask why?"

"I offered the professor the use of a cryptographic computer program we have developed to help him translate it. He agreed, so we downloaded all of his data from the codex. The program has been running since the day he...he...

"Yes. But you'll return it when you're done, please."

"Oh my, yes, of course," Danforth proclaimed. But I wasn't sure if I believed him.

"Do try the tea and scones," he indicated the silver tea service he had placed on the nightstand, "we have an excellent baker in our kitchen."

He left the tray and departed. The door slammed closed behind him with a heavy thud...the echo of which drowned out the gentle click that followed.

The second journal began:

"*2 January –*

I begin this new journal to mark the beginning of the new year. But while the year is new, the power within the Grimoire is ancient, primordial. I feel it radiating from the book in waves that grow stronger every day. Through my thin gloves, I can feel the images that the pages hold, the letters and lines and illustrations, and it is as if its power is soaking through my skin, seeping into my very blood.

The voice in my head is relentless now, with a stranglehold on my sanity. When I open the book, the only words I can see and hear and speak are those of Blaise, the scribe.

'Having fled to the western forest, Myrddin became known as the Green Man of the wood, a wizard living in seclusion among the animals and trees, with his true name all but passing from the lips of men. But spending his days communing with the life of the green was the greatest joy that Myrddin had ever known, and losing his name was a small price for such a gift.

Peasants from Vortigern's kingdom would sometimes stumble upon the Green Man as they hunted in the forest, and sometimes he would fill their sacks in exchange for news. In this way, Myrddin learned of the eventual victory of the Saxons in Briton, after many years of conflict. He heard, too, of the flight of cowardly King Vortigern to the north while abandoning his only son, Arturus (a bastard the king had inflicted upon his own daughter, Adhan), leaving the boy as a hostage of Hengist and Horsa.

The Saxon warlords held Arturus at Dinas Emir. They sent

riders in all directions to tell the world that the king's son would be sacrificed to Woden if the head of Vortigern was not delivered to them by the end of the summer solstice, only two weeks hence. All in the kingdom hoped that Arturus would be rescued but, alas, no champion had yet come forward and the sands in the glass would soon run out.'"

"*9 January –*

Druids did not write. They were a priestly order with an oral tradition and left behind no written record of their lives, just stories and rituals passed from master to acolyte. So one must wonder how this book—

'This threat to his young half-brother, and to the entire kingdom, prompted Myrddin to reclaim his name and return to the world of men, leaving his madness behind him.

He drew the Dragonsword from the Altar Stone and proceeded to Dinas Emir. He would have dealings, first with the Saxons, then with Vortigern. All would be put right. Then he would give the sword to Arturus so he may grow up to safeguard the kingdom from invaders and despots and dragons, and Myrddin could then return to his beloved green, retreating far from the mind and memory of men once more, for as long as the gods would allow.'"

"*15 January –*

My sleep is now fitful to the point of pointlessness. Each day, I find my progress stifled, but my understanding blooms full when I close my eyes each night and retreat into an unconscious state. But the understanding fades quickly upon awakening and is lost. That is why I moved into this room that has become my cell; only by breaking down the petty distinction between wakefulness and sleep will I find and keep the answers I seek."

"28 January –

I must remember to eat. Danforth says I do not look well and has expressed concern. But food has little interest for me now. I can feed only on the book. Yet the book is starving me; the voice in my head has gone silent."

"3 February –

Blaise has been quiet for weeks, but I continue to deteriorate, regardless. I can feel my blood screaming for me to release it. What happened to Myrddin? I must know, but the narrative has abandoned me. Perhaps I am no longer worthy to receive it."

"17 February –

It is often too difficult now to write down my thoughts. So this is my ironic notation of that condition for future reference, if a future I still may have."

"29 February –

Today is my birthday...Leap Day. As a leapling, I've celebrated only a quarter of my years alive in this world, making me much younger than I am. But I do not feel young anymore.

I have been cutting myself and using my blood to draw symbols on the stone wall of my room. But I do this without consciousness of my acts and am surprised on the mornings when new pictures have appeared and my wounds are reopened and raw. I wrap my hands in torn strips of linen that I have ripped from the bedding in order to close the cuts, and then I hide the bloody bandages in the suitcase beneath my cot.

I worry that my blood may fall into the wrong hands. It may have great power now. And I do not trust Danforth. I do not trust him at all."

"14 March –

All is not what it seems. I can feel the creature stirring. She is coming. Can I stop her? How? My blood is tainted, and my codex is missing. I will write to Loewenstein. He must know of this. Everyone must know. But perhaps it is too late, and I'm just a fool. Perhaps I should just say goodbye."

That was it...the last entry. My poor Wingate, unconscious in some asylum, had left his mind behind on these pages. What was there to be done? I would find Danforth, get back the third journal and head off for Sefton in the morning.

I crossed the room to leave but the door would not open. Stuck? No... locked.

Of course. Wingate's codex was missing. He never would have sought the assistance of a computer program to do his work. That was a bald-faced lie by that bald-headed magpie and I should have realized it immediately. Danforth had stolen the journal.

"Danforth!" I screamed through the thick oak door. "Danforth!"

There was no response. I could howl forever, but no one would hear through those impenetrable walls. I started to panic. The airless room felt like it was getting smaller. I began to sweat profusely. My breathing became labored. Then, a thought pushed its way forward.

Having caught on to Danforth's deceit, Wingate may have left a clue behind. Or a secret passage, a secret weapon. Something! I scanned the room for an alternate egress. I looked for a hole, or a drain, or a vent, but there was no way out. So I looked through his things again, and inside the desk drawer, and under the bed. I found nothing but dust and cobwebs.

By then my panic had transformed into determination. I re-read the journals, and then I stared at the symbols that Wingate had drawn on the wall in his own blood. I stared at them for a long time. I began to feel like they were calling to me. I pulled out his suitcase from beneath the cot. There were the linen strips coated in Wingate's dried blood. But what good would they be? Did they contain some sort of power or was that just Wingate's insane rambling?

As I contemplated the blood-stained rags laid out on the cot, I reached over and took Winnie's cigarette case and lighter off the nightstand. I took out a Dunhill, lit it, then put the case and lighter in my coat pocket, where I heard them clink against my phone. My cell phone. My smart little computer of a cell phone. Damn me for a fool.

Of course there was no cell service here (an unfortunate phrase, given my predicament), but in this day and age even an old castle has Wi-Fi if it sits on a university campus. I might be able to text or email someone for assistance, but to whom could I reach out? What would the authorities make of my tale of druids and blood rites and antediluvian gods? The only friend I had who would have believed me was now lying in a coma in Sefton. The police would probably want to lock me up in the room next to him, but I had to try nonetheless.

I found an unsecured internet connection and logged on. But before I knew it, my phone was no longer under my control. The face of a woman matching Wingate's description of The Morrigan appeared on the phone's tiny screen and spoke:

"I CALL OUT TO ALL WHO CAN HEAR ME! BRING THE DRAGONSWORD TO MY ACOLYTES OR I WILL ANNIHILATE YOU ALL!"

It may have been a computer virus of some sort. Or perhaps it was an angry warrior goddess fighting her way back into our world. Such was my situation that the latter seemed the more plausible explanation.

Danforth's computer must have completed the translation and, by doing so, had released The Morrigan, or at least her digital manifestation, into the world. The university's network was likely connected to the worldwide web, too, which meant that she could enter not just my phone, but every phone, laptop, tablet, desktop and server on the planet that was online at that moment. If that were true, she could instigate global chaos. But at least the goddess could not become corporeal without...without...

Danforth entered the room. He was not alone. He and his colleagues wore robes with the sigil that appeared on the door and gate of the library. I recognized it as the symbol on the cover of the *Grimoire* itself. As I was later to learn, it was the avatar of the crow, an insignia of the Druids' Morrigan cult whose sole purpose was to bring Graale, "the destroyer of worlds," back into our reality to destroy the one god.

Danforth's eyeglasses gleamed in the candlelight as he came at me with a knife of intimidating proportion and design. I backed up against the wall, wishing I was on the other side of it. Searching about for a weapon, I saw Wingate's bloody linen strips on the bed. Dried, the blood was useless. But maybe...

I swirled one of the bandages in the bedside teapot. With the blood moistened and thus revivified, I slapped the wet rag against the symbols on the wall. Suddenly, and impossibly, I found myself falling through the solid stone and landing flat on my face on the snowy ground outside the library.

Wingate had created a portal with his own blood, a blood tainted and fueled by the power of *The Morrigan's Grimoire*. He must have been imprisoned as I was and so escaped through the wall to...to do what?

My musings were interrupted by crazed cultists pouring out of the library and charging toward me. I leapt to my feet and ran. Then I saw it... the statue of King Arthur, standing in the middle of the quad. Wingate had tried to reach it before he was carted away. Why? I ran over to it and read the inscription stamped on its base: *"King Arthur wielding Excalibur, the Dragonsword."* Ah, well now.

I still had the wet bandage in my hand when I tried to pull the stone sword from Arthur's petrified grip. It drew out with ease, as if from a granite scabbard, but after seeing what Wingate's grimoire-infected blood had already accomplished, I cannot say I was surprised.

Upon being drawn forth, the Dragonsword transformed into gleaming steel and, when Danforth and the others approached me, I wheeled on them. In so doing, I nicked my hand on the razor sharp blade, due to my inexperience with such a weapon...or any weapon, for that matter. But the taste of my blood brought the sword to sudden life. It began to glow white and give off a droning hum that tickled the back of my neck. Danforth and his twisted cabal were blinded by the light and deafened by the din, and they all collapsed with spasmodic seizures of a grotesque nature, affording me the opportunity to make my unlikely escape.

The ice storm had ceased. The road was clear. I roared off toward Sefton in my rental car, with the Dragonsword by my side. It had turned back into silent stone. My palm was bleeding profusely from my self-inflicted wound, so, as I drove, I wrapped it with the wet strip I still held in my hand, not at all concerned that Wingate's blood was co-mingling with my own.

That was when my phone rang. Perhaps it was the doctor at Sefton, with news about Winnie. But when I answered, I heard a deep yet feminine voice with an Irish lilt.

"Wielder of the Dragonsword, return the sacred blade to my priests and your death will be quick and honorable. But defy me, and I will visit terrors upon you!"

I nearly drove off the road. But then I realized The Morrigan remained incorporeal, so what harm could she do me?

"Fuck you," I said, or words to that effect. Frankly, I was shocked by my own vulgarity.

She laughed.

"You have courage, human, and an equally admirable lack of restraint. But it shall avail you not on this foolish quest to rescue your friend, the mad old priest."

"Priest?"

"He is the last of Myrddin's bloodline and so is connected to me, to the book, and to the sword. His physical being is safely locked away and his mind and spirit are trapped in a prison of his own devising, so you will not be able to free either his body or his soul. Return the sword...return it and I will guarantee you a place of honor in the new world, when Graale comes."

"Why do you require the sword? You have no hands with which to brandish it."

"Not yet, but that condition will be addressed when my acolytes use it on the priest and summon me forth!"

"And then, what...you'll eat those fools, too?"

"Likely, yes."

"But not me, is that correct?"

"THAT IS CORRECT."

My wounded hand was throbbing now. "Fuck you," I explained again, this time liking the way it sounded. I'm sure Wingate would lecture me on the word's Germanic etymology, when I found him.

I hung up and drove on toward Sefton. On the way, I thought I saw crows circling overhead, but when I looked again, there was nothing in the grey sky but darkening clouds.

I made it to the hospital without further interruption.

"Hello, Dr. Loewenstein. We spoke on the phone earlier today. I'm, Dr. Mannerbund, Professor Wingate's physician here at Sefton. Welcome."

"Thank you, doctor. I'm anxious to see my friend, if you please."

"I'm sorry but we cannot allow him any visitors right now. He's undergoing treatment."

I wondered what sort of treatment a comatose non-responsive patient normally had to undergo.

"Yes, very well. But when can I see him?"

"We'll let you know. You can leave Professor Wingate's belongings here with us and return home for now."

"Belongings?"

"Yes, you recall I asked you to bring his things up from Mysticonic."

"What do you know of his belongings, and why would he need any such if he is currently unconscious?" I was growing concerned about Mannerbund's disposition.

"I thought that if he came into contact with some familiar objects from his life, it might bring him back to a conscious state. It's only a hypothesis, but worth a try."

My suspicions were growing exponentially. "No, sorry. I had to leave Mysticonic rather abruptly. I brought nothing."

"Nothing? Nothing he might have touched? A book, or—"

"Or a cigarette case?"

"Yes, or—"

"Or a sword, perhaps?" I studied his features to gauge his reaction.

"Yes, or a sword." Mannerbund face visibly relaxed. He would no longer have to maintain his façade and he seemed relieved.

He spoke into a walkie-talkie. "Go to lockdown." He looked at me and smiled. It wasn't a friendly smile.

"The Morrigan wants the Dragonsword, Loewenstein, and you will not refuse."

A pair of huge, brutish orderlies, with sloping brows and massive hands, grabbed me from behind and threw me into a padded cell. They would search my car for the sword and when they didn't find it, they'd return to inquire as to its whereabouts. And I doubted they would ask politely.

Wingate's room in the library was filled with despair, but this sterile, brightly lit cell was more disturbing by far. The claustrophobia it induced made my head ache, my heart race, and my panic rise. I concentrated on the throbbing in my wounded hand; the pain allowed me to focus and calm myself.

Sometime later, I'm not certain how long, Mannerbund came in. The orderlies (angry twins who I began to think of as Hengist and Horsa) followed him into the room, pushing a gurney with a towel folded on it.

"Where did you hide it?" Mannerbund asked, no longer smiling.

"I'll tell you what I told your goddess: fuck you."

At which point, Horsa beat me severely about the head and torso. When he paused, I stalled to regain my composure.

"What is so important about a sword?" I gasped, feigning ignorance and spitting blood.

"The Morrigan requires Wingate and the Dragonsword to complete the ritual, so she can enter our world. But I'm sure you knew that already, didn't you?"

Mannerbund unfolded the towel to reveal sharp-edged medical instruments laid out on the stainless steel gurney. Their blades sparkled in the sickly, yellowish-green fluorescent light. My sphincter began to tighten. The twins, their respite concluded, pulled me up to my feet.

"Before you start in with further unpleasantness, could I impose on you for a glass of water?" I asked innocently.

"Will you give us the sword?" persisted Mannerbund.

"Yes. I don't need to be vivisected. Just some water, please."

Mannerbund nodded to Hengist, and so he went out and returned with a pill cup filled with water. When he handed it to me, I poured the water onto the rag which was still wrapped around my hand and then punched the behemoth in the throat as hard as I could. He buckled. I then took the palm of my hand and drove his nasal cartilage into his brain. Now where had I learned to do that?

The other one, Horsa, came at me but I ducked, snatched a scalpel off the gurney and plunged it deeply into the orbit of his right eye. Vitreous fluid squirted out of the socket in a thick stream, and then my torturer fell to the floor like a sack of rocks.

Mannerbund grabbed surgical scissors and plunged them into my chest, knocking me back. But the scissor blades were stopped by the cigarette case in my breast pocket and just stuck there. Mannerbund went white-eyed and turned pale. I pulled out the scissors and put their point up against his carotid artery.

"Why don't we go find my friend and then we can all depart here together, instead of in pieces," I whispered. He nodded.

I retrieved the scalpel from Horsa's skull, grabbed Mannerbund by the scruff of his neck and pushed him out of the cell in front of me.

"Really, Dr. Loewenstein, this violence isn't—"

"Please shut up, doctor." I poked him in the small of the back with the scalpel, but just a bit. He understood my meaning and we started down the hall.

As we proceeded, I considered my recent behavior.

Fuck you, I had said. Twice...no, thrice. Out loud. But I did not commonly indulge in profanity, or even slang for that matter. *Courage* and *a lack of restraint*, The Morrigan had said of me. And just now I demonstrated an aptitude for physical violence that I had heretofore never exhibited. What was happening to me?

Perhaps my sudden bloodlust and martial skills were a consequence of the growing infection in my hand caused by mixing my own bodily fluids with Wingate's ancestral demon blood, corrupted as it was by the power of *The Morrigan's Grimoire*. Either that or I was having a complete and total nervous breakdown. Such was my situation that the former seemed the more plausible explanation.

Whatever the cause, I felt stronger, more confident, and less tethered by the restraints of civilization. And what was more, I liked it. But I didn't particularly like that I liked it.

We reached Wingate's room. There were two guards at his door, both wearing hospital whites bearing the small crow insignia on their breasts.

"Stand down," whispered Mannerbund, at my insistence.

I had them precede us into the room. There lay poor Winnie...spread-eagled on a bed, bare-chested, strapped down and tied to the railings, with an IV drip in his arm and his vacant eyes staring at nothing. My anger grew.

"Untie him," I growled at the guards, keeping the scalpel at Mannerbund's throat for them to see, "and put him in that wheelchair."

After they did so, I lost consciousness. When I revived, I saw Mannerbund cowering in the corner, with the guards dead on the floor and blood on my hands...and on my pants...and my shirt. There was blood everywhere, in fact, but none of it was mine. I was nauseated and tempted to either vomit or scream, but I did neither. Instead, I prodded Mannerbund back into action and had him wheel Wingate out to my car. He loaded the professor into the passenger seat. Then I pushed Mannerbund into the trunk and sped away.

I stopped to pick up the Dragonsword, which I had buried in the woods on the outskirts of town before arriving at Sefton. I helped Mannerbund out of the trunk and, after briefly considering splitting him in twain, I put the sword in the trunk and sent him running off. My rage had receded and I was coming back to myself. I looked over at the unmoving Wingate next to me and pulled the blanket further up on his lap. Then I set out for the turnpike, heading west.

We drove through the night. Upon our arrival in Madison the next day, I picked up some items from Winnie's home, including cash, a deck of cards, a case of cigarettes, a bottle of brandy, and as many of Winnie's books as I could fit into the car. From my apartment, I recovered the .38 handgun given to me long ago by a disreputable friend. I then smashed my cellphone to bits with the gun's grip and stole a car after dumping the rental into a lake. We headed off, driving further west.

We arrived at a rustic cabin in the wooded mountains of northern Colorado, near Rockton. It had been left to me by an elderly couple, now deceased, with whom I once shared an afternoon and a story some many years past...a lifetime ago, it seems. And that is where we now reside, Winnie and I. The cabin is entirely off the grid, as they say, and its complete lack of connectedness has allowed us to escape The Morrigan's sight, at least so far. I have fortified both the structure and the surrounding grounds against human incursion, in case they pick up our trail.

Most critically, I succeeded in using Wingate's notes and his blood to summon *The Morrigan's Grimoire* to this remote place. It appeared on our kitchen table just as suddenly as it once had in the bowels of the Mysticonic Library. By so doing, I have kept it out of the malevolent grasp of the goddess and her death cult.

Still, The Morrigan's numbers grow daily. Each day, she spills out into the world in her digital form; her powers expand, and the weak-minded come into her service. Soon, she'll have her tendrils into every nook and cranny of life on this planet. Markets will crash, planes will fall from the sky, missiles will launch by mistake...strife and chaos will prevail. Until then, I keep Wingate and the sword beyond her grasp, so she is denied a gateway back into our reality. In this way, the coming of Graale is postponed, one day at a time.

And so I spend each of those days shooting whatever crows I see. And I smoke Winnie's excellent cigarettes and drink his fine brandy, and I read his books, desperately trying to learn enough about his life's work to make the *Grimoire* give up its remaining secrets. And I watch over my friend's empty body and pray he will return to it one day so the Green Man within him can enact a plan to save the world.

But my prayers have gone unanswered. Instead, I wake up every morning and stare at the Dragonsword, a blade that men once called Excalibur. It whispers to me and I seriously consider using it to carve the *Grimoire's* sacred sigils into Wingate's sleeping flesh, to perform the summoning ritual and then revel in the carnage to follow.

Every hour of every day, the *Grimoire's* poison burns through my infected blood and pushes me towards Ragnarok, and every day I resist the siren's call, distracting myself by transcribing all that has transpired onto these pages of Winnie's last remaining journal, so that these events are not lost and forgotten.

But I don't know how much longer I can hold out before I am finally overcome, either from the blood within or the forces without. How long do we have before we are out of time? How long before Danforth or Mannerbund show up on our doorstep?

My god, how long is left...

...ERE GRAALE COMES?

GRAALE, THE DARK GOD WHO LIVES BEYOND THE STARS, WHO CAME INTO BEING BEFORE ALL THE OTHER GODS THAT FOLLOWED THEREAFTER...

...GRAALE, THE FIRST AND THE LAST, THE ALPHA AND OMEGA, THE MAKER AND DESTROYER OF WORLDS...

Gods Out of Time

H.P. Lovecraft meets Merlin. That was the idea. I wanted to write a horror story, and I wanted to adapt an Arthurian myth, so I decided to go for both in one shot. God, what an idiot.

I have no particular affinity for horror, so that was one of the reasons I wanted to write a horror story...meet the challenge, face my fears, or some such nonsense. I also felt this collection would be incomplete, genre-wise, if I didn't try to include one.

When casting about for a horrific idea, the first thing I thought about was Lovecraft. Howard Phillips Lovecraft (August 20, 1890 – March 15, 1937) was not only a hugely influential writer at the dawn of the twentieth century, he became an entire sub-genre of horror unto himself—sui generis—with a style, a philosophy, and a set of definable tropes and themes that are recognizably present in much of modern horror literature and cinema. So Lovecraft could provide a ramshackle haunted house within which I could comfortably reside, since it was so familiar to me and would likely be so to a genre-reading audience, even if they didn't know where they recognized it from.

Then I started researching the canon of Arthurian mythology for an appropriate story to...well, appropriate. The more I looked into the demonic backstory on Merlin, the more Lovecraftian he felt, so I focused on his origin and rewrote whatever I felt like to fit, as so many other writers had done over the past thousand years or so. Unfortunately, I got bogged down in minutiae and, since I was also avoiding the whole problem of being "scary," I got unbearably blocked and just stopped writing altogether. But I'm a stubborn man by nature, so surrender was not going to happen...at least not for a good long while.

A good long while later and here we are. The breakthrough happened when my son told me not to try and be scary.

"You're not scary, dad. Just be creepy. You can do creepy."

Gee thanks, Matt.

Afterward

And now that our journey through the marvelous spiral is done, it's time to say thank you and bid you a sincere *adieu*. Loewenstein offered a wordy fare-thee-well, but I don't have the space. Emmett just grunted and said, "piss off, pal"...or words to that effect.

Well, that's my story anyway and I'm sticking to it.

Special Thanks

To Neil Gaiman – and to Jim Thompson, Hunter S. Thompson, J.R.R. Tolkien, H.P. Lovecraft, T.H. White, Werner Heisenberg, Isaac Asimov, Edith Hamilton, Harlan Ellison, Edgar Rice Burroughs, Bruno Bettelheim, Jacob Bernoulli, Friedrich Nietzsche, Wassily Kandinsky, Clint Eastwood, Donald Westlake, Bob Dylan, Philip K. Dick, David Ives, Peter David, Pablo Picasso, Sam Peckinpah, Kurt Vonnegut, Karl Jung, Frank Gilroy, George Carlin, Jack Kirby, Stan Lee, Alan Moore, Mark Twain, John Wayne, Joss Whedon, Jonathan Coulton, Joseph Campbell, Kevin Smith, Michael Chabon, Theodore Sturgeon, Siegel & Shuster, and many, many others – for the inspiration;

To Brian J. McCarthy, for being that one teacher;

To Susan Kaufman, the gifted artist and friend, for providing the haunting illustrations, both for this book and for my home;

To my "beta testers," those friends, relatives and colleagues (like Mike Barrett, Steve Cosares, Mike D'Andrea, Judy Fremont, JoAnn Gredell, Lloyd Jassin, Lorrie Krebs, Herb Sevush, Steve Sevush, Tobe Sevush, Pam Weinstock, and the Crane Pool Forum) who read early drafts of these stories, for giving me encouraging and indispensable feedback ...and to those who ignored me completely and hoped I'd go away (you know who you are);

To those editors, like Wendy Delmater, Fred Coppersmith and Jason Brock, for giving me a shot...and to those who didn't; and

To the Mets, for failing to take up much of my free time until I was done writing this, and then winning the pennant for the first time in 15 years;

To one and all, I thank you

Biographies

RALPH SEVUSH, ESQ. (Author) is a graduate of Stony Brook University and the Cardozo School of Law. He began his career in motion-picture marketing, sales, distribution, and script development for New Line Cinema and other NY-based film companies. Later, as an entertainment attorney, he worked on the Broadway productions of *BIG-the Musical, Fool Moon,* and *God Said, "HA!",* before coming to the Dramatists Guild in 1997. He has been the Guild's co-Executive Director and General Counsel since 2005.

As a writer, in addition to the stories in *Spira Mirablis,* his credits include: *Savage Cinema,* a film review column for *Worlds of If...*magazine (1983), and *Little One, Goodbye,* an award-winning play produced by the Tada! Theater, the Enchanted Players of New Jersey, the Lower East Side Tenement Museum, and the Innovative Stages Company (1994-1996). The play later earned him acceptance into the BMI/Lehman-Engel Musical Theater Librettists Workshop (1999). He has also authored countless essays for *The Dramatist* magazine over the past 20 years, primarily on copyright, free speech, and the theater industry.

Mr. Sevush was born and raised in Brooklyn, and now resides in the wilds of Westchester, with his wife, two children, two dogs and a frog.

SUSAN KAUFMAN (Illustrator): The pen and ink drawings in *Spira Mirablis* were created by New York-based artist Susan Kaufman, whose preferred atmosphere is the fog and mist of Victorian London. She uses ink and brush, cut paper and old photographs to create layered works with an old fashioned and haunted aesthetic, finding ways to depict the things that disappear if you look too closely, or that shouldn't be but are.

This is her first collaboration with Ralph Sevush.

You can see more of her work at www.srkaufman.com, where she presents shadow-box images of the uncanny.

taQ'Lut* PRESS (publisher) is a New York-based independent publisher specializing in genre fiction... offering weird stories for a weirder world. See our website at www.taqlutpress.com and contact us at taqlutpress@gmail.com

*taQ Lut [adj, TOK; noun,-LOOT] (origin: Klingon) - weird stories

Illustrations

Emmett, Joey, & the Beelz

La Joie de Vivre
or, Picasso & the Satyr

A Love of Mine

Illustrations

Mad Gilly & the Were-Bear

The Firebird: A Fairy Tale

Confessions of the Last Ronin

Illustrations

Survivors in the Dark

Gods Out of Time

www.ingramcontent.com/pod-product-compliance
Lightning Source LLC
Chambersburg PA
CBHW050943120626
46552CB00001B/351